# DRIFTMETAL

## Segment One

*J.C. Staudt*

# DRIFTMETAL
## Segment One

*Driftmetal* is a work of fiction. Names, characters, organizations, places, events, and incidents either are products of the author's imagination or are used fictitiously. Any resemblance to actual persons, living or dead, events, or locales is entirely coincidental.

ISBN-13: 978-1512189438
ISBN-10: 151218943X

First Edition

Printed in the United States of America

*Book design by J.C. Staudt*

*To the Legendary Heroes of Cataclysmic Fire,*
*for always adventuring.*

# 1

I opened my leg and dug around inside, trying to figure out what was wrong with the blasted thing. If I didn't get a reflex response soon, the battered old hovercell in which I was imprisoned was going to carry me down to the Churn and get shredded like a tin can in a blender. Gilfoyle's thugs had roughed me up pretty good, ripping out my insides like they wanted to sell me for spare parts, and what was left of me was not cooperating.

I should start by telling you that centuries ago, this world shattered, leaving its core raw and exposed. I don't know why it happened, or how, but chunks of land have been floating through the skies on veins of driftmetal ever since. One of those chunks, a drift-town called Bannock, was getting away from me. I could still see the big floater gliding along in the skyward realm like a storm cloud, its rocky black edges haloed in the yellowy shimmer of street lamps. I wanted to be up there again, enjoying myself at the tavern, floating away with the biggest haul of my life. That haul would've brought in enough chips to make my mom blush and my dad question why he'd ever doubted me.

Mining platforms whipped by outside the hovercell window, their border beacons strobing like runway lights on an airfield. I wedged my heel in at the base of the door and poked around in my thigh with my makeshift tools—a pair of tweezers and a chicken bone I'd sharpened to a point with the edge of my boot. Not my proudest moment.

When the hovercell hit the nearflow, the whole thing started to shake. Dust and particles and tiny floaters began to pummel the hull like popcorn kernels in a vacuum cleaner while the hovercell's quartet of displacer engines struggled to keep her steady. The thing was shaking so bad I could hear my boot rattling on the bench across the room—so bad I snapped off the tip of the chicken bone inside my leg. I tossed the rest of the bone aside and cursed the thugs for having put me in this situation. No sense of humor, those guys. Never mind that I'd brought it upon myself.

Yes, my life of crime had finally caught up with me, but I had to hand it to Gilfoyle's henchpersons all the same; they were no law-lovers. Instead of calling up the Civs to come drag me off to prison, they'd taken matters into their own hands. The Churn was active tonight, and staging my death as an accident was a clever way to get rid of me. It was too bad they'd made a classic mistake; they should've finished the job themselves. Rookies.

The hovercell rumbled louder. I cursed out loud and pounded my knee, using my hand like a mallet. I stuck a finger inside, cursed again when I got it pinched in the machinery. There was a pop and a spark, and my tweezers pinged away and bounced across the floor. A second later the solenoid shot from my heel and slammed the latch, chipping the door open enough for me to shoulder it the rest of the way.

A surge of momentary pride swelled in my chest. These hovercells looked solid, but they had weaknesses, and I knew every one. Before I went out into the surface storm, I glanced back at the chicken bone, the tweezers, and my boot. *I'll get another boot*, I decided.

I slid out of my trapezoidal box and let myself dangle by the arms, feeling very much like a limp noodle hanging from the fold-out panel of a take-out carton. The hovercell was dropping fast and my stomach was doing somersaults, but I'd gotten out of these things before and I knew just where to place my hands and feet. Like a kid on the monkey bars, I swung forward and hooked my leg onto the coolant pipe running along the underside of the hovercell. When I felt the crook of my knee come to rest, I let go with my hands. I'm no gymnast, but upside down is a strange place to be with displacer engines pushing a thousand tons of gravel-choked air a second past your face.

Yeah, I pretty much had the hovercell right where I wanted it.

I crunched up, because back then my abs weren't so much to scoff at, and took hold of a fuel line. I had about a minute and a half—maybe less—before the hovercell reached the Churn. I pulled myself up until my face was inches from the control panel, then triggered my eyelight and was pleased to find that it still worked like a charm. The focused beam of light followed my darting pupil as I scanned the panel for the component in question: the Lift Processor.

Reversing the thrust wasn't the hard part. The hard part was not getting shot into the Churn like a billiard ball when the engines multiplied power. That meant that before I altered the Lift Processor, I needed a way back inside the hovercell. I pounded the heel of my palm into the access hatch until I could see the silver metallic gleam of telerium through the skin of my hand. The hatch was dented, but I wasn't through yet. It left me wishing I had something to blast it open with. I would've, if the thugs hadn't ripped out all my sweet tech.

It took another thirty seconds of bashing before I sent the access hatch sailing up into the hovercell and clattering to the floor within. When I squinted at the control panel, the green beam that shot out of my eye severed one connection and joined another. I felt the engine noise start to build as I clambered beneath the pipes, hoisting myself back inside. Through the open hatch I could see the Churn boiling below me, a seismic sea of liquefied stone and grit and gas and sand and metal, the leftovers of a planet that hadn't seen a year without thousands of quakes like this since centuries before I was born.

The hovercell's descent slowed gradually, like a rubber band reaching its limit. It hovered in place for a lingering moment that dragged on so long I thought I'd cut the wrong connection. Then it began to slog upward. The side door was still hanging open, bumping the floor every few seconds like the wing of a wounded bird, refusing to catch on the latch I'd obliterated with my solenoid heel. I reclaimed my lost boot and made a silent exclamation. *Won't need another pair of boots after all.* I picked up the tweezers and stuffed them into a pocket. *Can't hurt to keep these*, I thought. *Unibrow ain't gonna pluck itself.*

We were rising faster now, me and my erstwhile deathtrap. I waited until I saw the first mining platform go by, then the second. We rose up out of the nearflow into clearer skies. When I saw the third platform, I sprang the door and jumped for it, hitting the deck and rolling through the landing. I looked up and watched the hovercell continue rising overhead. It smacked into the next mining platform, careened sideways, and crashed into a skid along the topside. Even from thirty feet below, the metal-on-metal scraping was loud enough to make me cover my ears. When the hovercell reached the far edge of the platform, it tipped off the side and dropped like a stone.

"That's gonna be bad," I said, pleased with myself.

It was bad. The engines were running full-bore all the way to the Churn. I hadn't left the stabilizers active, because... well, I guess I hadn't thought about it. Why did I care what happened to the ride after I got off? A hot orange flower bloomed below me. There came a dull roar that peaked above the rumble of the Churn. The night was black-and-blue again, except for the yellow pools of light from the drift-towns passing above. I found Bannock, which had floated past my left shoulder and was fading into the distance. What was the name of that tavern again?

"Mulrainy Jikes."

A dark-skinned visitor in a long purple duster and a wide-brimmed hat stood before me on the platform. My name is *Mulroney Jakes*, but this guy's weird accent made it sound... weird. The solenoid was jammed, still sticking a foot out from my heel, so I stood there like an improperly-built scarecrow and shrugged.

"That was a valiant effort," said the dark-skinned man, "but I'm afraid I can't let you get away that easily."

"You'd better make it harder than the last guys did," I said.

I'd never seen this guy before, but I knew by his smug demeanor that he was some kind of law-loving bounty hunter, one of the Civvies' freelance agents. The thugs had gotten the best of me, but that was only because there'd been half a dozen of them. By contrast, there were as many of me as there were of this guy; pretty decent odds, in my book.

The velcro flap over my thigh was still hanging open. I slapped it shut and rubbed the seal to make sure it was tight.

The dark-skinned man must've been getting a good look at my inner workings before I noticed. The less he knew about those, especially in the condition I was in, the better.

There was a line of hovertrucks parked at the far side of the platform, mining vehicles made for hauling heavy loads. Don't be so pretentious as to think this was my idea of a luxury ride. Any vehicle that could get me up to Bannock and back to my streamboat was fair game, at this particular juncture. I had to get across that platform. But first, there was the small matter of this melodramatic do-gooder in my way.

"You've terrorized these miners for the last time, *Jikes*," said the dark-skinned man, proving that he was indeed a melodramatic do-gooder.

"Everybody wants to be a hero," I said, rolling my eyes. I stomped down hard to shove the solenoid back where it belonged. The metal clangor resounded along the platform, and the landing lights around the border gave a flicker.

The dark-skinned man didn't have time for small talk. I felt his grapplewire wrap around my legs before I realized he'd shot the thing. He yanked hard on the line, pulling my feet out from under me. I hit the deck and started sliding toward him. He extended a boot, doing me the courtesy of providing a brake for my momentum. I shoved off sideways with my hands and forced myself into a slanted roll, twisting counter-clockwise to unwrap my legs. I tried to grab the wire, but when I came around on the last twist it ripped free of my calf and took a nice chunk of flesh and pants with it.

I rolled to a stop in an almost-seated position. The man shot his wire again, but I raised a hand to shield myself. The grappler pierced my palm and came to rest within an inch of my eye. When he yanked on the line, the spring-loaded prongs flicked out and bit into the back of my hand.

He began to reel me in, so I turned down my heels and let him lift me onto my feet like a water-skier. I went airborne just before I reached him, straightening out like a wooden plank and plunging my feet into that law-loving face of his. He would've gotten a solenoid through the skull too, if I'd been able to trigger the blasted thing on cue. I followed through the kick, intending to land on my feet and send him sprawling. Problem was, I was practically holding the guy's hand, so we tumbled across the deck together like a pair of broken chairs.

I managed to end up underneath him somehow. The grappler was still tugging my palm toward his wrist, its motor chugging like a stuck wind-up toy. Lucky for me, his brain was still knocking around in his skull. All he could do was give me a woozy stare as I shoved him off me and worked my hand free of the grappler.

I took off toward the hovertrucks, my hand a mess of bloodstained metal, sliced veins flopping out like thin plastic tubing. With the same hand, I punched through the driver's side window and climbed into the first hovertruck, wiping glass shards off the seat.

After a moment of fiddling, the engines growled to life, and the hovertruck lurched and rose. More *staggered* than rose, really. With the dark-skinned man getting to his feet on the platform below, it felt like I was driving through a vat of maple syrup. *Come on come on come on come on.* These things were easy to hotwire, but they moved slower than cold boogers.

I should probably mention that I came up working as a mechanic in my dad's shop. That was before I learned how to make a dishonest living. *Dear old dad*, I thought, without missing him one bit.

I heard the undercarriage clank as the dark-skinned man's grappler bit through the truck bed. The hovertruck faltered and

J.C. Stout

the man was floating up, up on his line, holding onto his hat while his purple duster slapped at his knees. I lost sight of him under me, cursing the hovertruck for its lack of see-through flooring. I'm a good driver, and I can fight, but fighting and driving at the same time is a feat best left to stuntmen and cityfolk.

I shuffled through the glove box, searching the cockpit for something heavy. I could hear the soft metallic clinks of hands and feet along the chassis. A shame I hadn't gotten the dark-skinned man's name, since I liked being able to brag about who I'd killed. I took off a boot and kissed it. When the man's arm came through the open window, I grabbed his wrist and punched the grappler through the sole of my boot, triggering the prongs. Then I kicked the door open and cut the engine.

I bailed, using the boot as a step and holding onto the wire like a rappelling line. The dark-skinned man writhed against the door frame, my weight holding his arm through the window. The winch inside his forearm began to smoke as it tried to reverse the direction. Which it did, after a couple seconds. *Shucks. That did* not *go like I wanted it to.* Next I knew, I was being hauled *up* toward the truck. Now the engine was off, and the truck was coming *down.*

I let go of the wire and fell. I hit the platform from two stories up, an awkward landing that made my teeth rattle like pebbles in a landslide. The hovertruck was listing sideways and falling past the platform, fast. I could see the dark-skinned man, caught against the underside with nowhere to go, my boot gliding up toward him on the wire. There was a rush of wind as the truck tumbled past, and then he was gone.

When the hovertruck hit the Churn, the fireball wasn't as big or impressive as the hovercell's had been. Just an uninspired puff of flame and a brief column of gray smoke that blew away

8

in the wind below the first platform. The dark-skinned man's hat drifted down and swayed to rest in front of me. It had been a shame to ruin a good pair of boots, but at least I'd gotten an ugly hat out of the deal. *A fitting end to the life of another law-lover*, I thought.

The next hovertruck in line was just as cumbersome to drive as the first, but it had the benefit of being lighter by one law-lover. I tailed Bannock for a while, following in the drift-town's wake until I could land without causing a scene. The guys in the crow's nest could suck on my solenoid if they wanted to clear me first. I knew they were just doing their jobs, but I didn't care about their jobs. I'd been avoiding the life of an honest working man for years. And I'd been away too long to fool with procedure; I had to get back to her.

The town was a clockwork mass of sprawling gothic architecture and spooky manor houses as old as the patch of ground Bannock had been ripped away from. In the ages since, the inhabitants had built all the way out to the edges in some places. For the less faint of heart, there were side-bolted apartments overlooking the Churn.

I was a wanted man, but I made my way through the cobbled streets as though I wasn't. The stream was whipping my hair around my face as I came around to the edge of the floater, and there she was.

*Ostelle*, my rusty clunker of a streamboat. Gorgeous as the day she was born, if a little worse for the wear. I came aboard and entered the captain's quarters to find it rank with a sour-smelling crowd. My crew. Everything went quiet when I entered the room.

"Why are there so many people in here?" I wanted to know.

"Cause we're havin' a meeting. Where you been all day, ya lackwit? And what's with the stupid hat?"

My dear old dad, always the charmer.

I flipped the old man an obscene gesture. "I've been getting pinched and almost beaten to dust in the Churn. The hat's a souvenir. Where've *you* been?"

"Well shoot, son, I been right here, runnin' things while you were out playing dress-up. Why didn't you bluewave us?"

"Couldn't, on account of they stole all my tech. I could've been rotting away in a Civvy prison, for all you knew. I've been gone a whole night and day and you couldn't send *one* guy after me?"

"I thought you done took off with one of them tavern wenches and left us," dad said, nonchalant.

"You know I'd never leave my boat on purpose, dad."

"*Your* boat? Who keeps this bucket of driftmetal together, is it you? Cause last time I checked—"

"Alright, shut up. *Our* boat."

"Cap'n Jakes?"

"Yeah," my dad and I both said at the same time. We glared at each other, then at the man who'd spoken.

Mr. Leigam Irkenbrand hesitated, his beetled eyes darting back and forth between us. He was the boat's bluewave radioman; our mouth in the stream. He had been frail and thin, even back then, with a prominent cleft chin, a small nose and a thick head of gray locks pulled back into a tight ponytail. "Marshals are on the comm. Chatter about a couple of hovertrucks reported missing."

Dad looked at me. Every crewmember in the room looked at me.

I shrugged. "Yeah, it was me."

I'd expected the place to erupt with cheers and smiles, but the news only brought silence.

"Sounds like you're in a bit of trouble, son," Dad said. "Didn't run off with no tavern wench after all. What'd you haul in?"

"Nothing," I said. "Except for this hat. I was close to bringing in something really big this time."

Expectant silence became murmured disappointment.

"The marshals are asking if we have any information on the thefts," said Leigam.

"One's parked outside town," I said. "The other... they ain't gonna find the other."

Dad was irked. "Get below, son. Mr. Sarmiel, make ready to lift off. Stations!"

I made my way belowdecks, hungry as a dog and still aching, my bloody hand in need of patching and my left leg due for a tune-up. Merton Richter and Dorth Littage were stationed at the coal furnace, doing more sitting than shoveling. As soon as they saw me, they started pretending otherwise.

"Slackers," I said as I passed. "Liftoff soon. I'll kick your teeth in if we fall behind because of you jackwagons."

"Aye, cap," they said.

Merton thumbed over his shoulder and gave me a knowing look. "Cook's in the galley."

I frowned at him and trudged off in that direction.

"There's my sweet little boy," said the cook when I sat down. "What's with that dreadful hat?"

"Hey, Ma."

She leaned in, pinched my chin between two wet, floury fingers, and puckered up. I obliged her, then nodded out of her grasp. My mother, as beautiful and terrifying a woman as ever sailed the stream.

"You must be hungry," she said, returning to her work. "You missed dinner last night, and you didn't come home for breakfast or lunch today. Or dinner, either, come to think of it. This town isn't *that* big, Mull."

The guilt-trips never stopped. *When am I gonna get away from these people?* "You'll notice by the hole in my hand that I kinda got into some trouble," I pointed out.

She glanced over her shoulder, frowned, clucked her tongue. "What'd you bring in?"

I slumped my shoulders. "Not a blasted thing."

"You should be with the Doc, not down here," she said, hiding her disappointment with nagging.

"Dad mutinied again. Took command of the ship and told me to hide below until we shove off."

Ma huffed. "I'll call Doctor Ditmarus. Your father, I swear... we're supposed to be retired. Doesn't that man know how to take a moment's rest?"

I resisted the urge to point out what a hypocritical statement that was, coming from my mile-a-minute mom. Instead I said, "Sometimes I think Dad would like it if I got pinched. For good."

A moment's hesitation. "Don't be silly," Mom said, shoving a long whisk handle into her wrist port and whipping the bowl of batter like it deserved the punishment. "He loves you."

"Don't feed me that crap," I said. "You're a better cook than that."

She called Doctor Ditmarus on the intercom and set the bowl aside. "Someone's a little grumpy tonight," she said. "Go lie down and wait for him."

The whisk shed drops of batter as she waved me away.

I crossed into the crew cabin and set my ugly new hat down on a barrel. Then I pulled off my lone remaining boot and flung myself onto a spare bunk. My mind drifted to the medallion. *My* medallion. Life would be different if I ever got my hands on it.

I felt the turbines rumble down my spine. My stomach heaved as the boat pitched off and caught the stream. Building a good boat isn't just a matter of throwing a few scraps of driftmetal together. It has to be balanced. It has to have the right ingots in the right places, size and mass and purity, all in equal proportions. My *Ostelle*, she was a good boat. Just because Dad had built most of her for me didn't make her any less mine. I'd financed the endeavor, after all.

Speak of the devil, Dad's voice came over the intercom. "They're stopping us. The Civs want to search the boat. Mull, if you're somewhere where you can hear me, make yourself scarce."

*The marshals caught us?* I thought. *Not a chance.* Ostelle *can run and gun against anything the Civs could ever throw at her. Why wouldn't Dad just haul it out of here and leave them in the dust? Unless... he's making it easy for them to get to me.*

I was the only one in the crew cabin. There was something eerie about being alone. Maybe it was that I *felt* alone. Abandoned. *But he just told me to hide. Doesn't that mean he wants to keep me safe?*

Metal planks on the deck above shrieked under the weight of footsteps. I shouldered a set of webgear and darted into the galley, where Ma was laboring away at dinner as if there weren't half a dozen Civvy marshals coming aboard to take her only son into custody. When she turned to look at me, there was something strange in her eyes. Sorrow? No, that wasn't it.

"Better get out of sight," she said. "Where do you think you'll hide?"

Looking at my mother then, I realized it wasn't sorrow I saw in her eyes. It was betrayal. I went numb. I backed away. *How could you?* I almost said. *How much did they have to pay you to turn me in?* I could hear the footsteps spreading fore and aft, crossing decks and clunking down stairs.

The flecker was in my hand before I reached the furnace room. Two marshals were questioning Merton and Dorth as the crewmen leaned on their shovels, enjoying the break. I burst into the room and fired an erratic barrage, adrenaline pounding in my chest. All four men held up their hands to shield themselves. The flecker particles melted over them, searing away synthetic flesh like a hair dryer over butter.

With their skin out of the way, I could see that both marshals were heavily augmented, but that was no surprise. I kept shooting until I saw a clear path, then bolted past them. I heard them stumbling after me like a gaggle of anodized skeletons, screaming. I flew up the stairs and across the deck, but stopped short at the railing.

There were four Civvy sloops and a cruiser docked to my *Ostelle*. More than a score of them had come aboard, decked out in the red-and-tans of the Civil Regency Corps. I couldn't help but feel honored by the show of force.

"Drop it and come forward, nice and easy," said their commanding officer, a dark-haired mustachioed man I knew as Captain Ludolf Kupfer, the biggest law-lover of them all.

I didn't budge. "Ah, Kupfer. Isn't this an unexpected surprise? How nice of you to drop in and say hello."

Don't judge me. Sometimes you have to match a law-lover's smugness with a little smugness of your own. Well... you don't have to. But it's more fun that way.

Kupfer gave me a pained grimace, as if my greeting had been cliché enough to hurt him physically. "We've collected evidence that leads us to believe you're responsible for the deaths of as many as eleven missing persons, including three security personnel employed by a Mr. Alastair Gilfoyle as part of his Churn-mining operation. I'm afraid you'll have to come with me."

*Thirteen*, I would've said. *I'm responsible for the deaths of* thirteen *missing persons.* I wanted to thank Kupfer for underestimating my murder tally, but I couldn't have opened my mouth without correcting him. Plus, I knew better than to put myself at odds with the two dozen rifles his marshals were pointing in my direction.

*In my defense, the Churn was what did the killing*, I could've said, but didn't. I thought of the dark-skinned man, his funny accent and the equally funny look of terror he'd had on his face while he was falling. And Gilfoyle, that balding, cane-wielding, gold-ring-wearing rotten apple of a mining tycoon who still had my medallion. His medallion. *My...* medallion.

I looked around at my crew, standing off at the fringes of the conflict, cowering behind the marshals like children behind their mothers' skirts. I was pretty sure I knew then what Dad's little meeting had been about; why everyone had gone silent when I'd walked into the captain's quarters. They'd decided it was time to vote me off the boat. My crew was no longer mine.

*'You're rubbing mud on your cheeks instead of growing a beard,'* my dear old Dad always used to say. It was his way of pointing out when I was trying to shortcut things instead of taking the time to do them right. I felt like I could've said that to him right about then. If he wanted me gone, why hadn't he just told me so instead of letting these law-lovers do his dirty work for him?

"I'm sorry, son." Speak of the devil again, Dad emerged from the captain's quarters and closed the doors behind him. Wind played at the wisps of graying brown hair that had come loose from his tieback. His face was stern and cold as always, but I could see his age lines more in that moment than I ever had before.

"You *did* betray me," I said. "How much did it cost them to earn a law-loving keister like yours?"

"No, I didn't betray you, son. But I *am* letting this happen. The boys and I have decided we're going straight, and I knew you wouldn't agree with it."

My heart sank into my stomach and boiled there. I felt my eyes go wide and start to water. The wind was so strong I could feel the drips running sideways along my face like rain on a fast window. I wasn't crying, but I was worried it looked that way. "You're bloody right I wouldn't agree," I said, trying not to shout. The marshals and their guns were the only things keeping me from blowing a gasket. "You can't make a decision like that without me, Dad. You can't take her away from me."

I felt like a kid again, a spoiled child stamping his foot to get his way. I wasn't just some kid though, and *Ostelle* wasn't a toy. She was my life. From the moment she'd gone airworthy a few months back, I'd been dreaming of the hundreds of new capers and scams I was going to pull. I had things I wanted to get done, and curse Dad if he thought I was going to do them any way but mine.

"There's good, honest money to be made in privateering," Dad was saying. "We've acquired ourselves an official Regency sanction, and being sanctioned by the Regency has its perks."

"I ain't no bootlicker, Dad."

Dad snorted and spat something onto the deck. "See, I knew you'd never go for it. Some time in lockup will do you good, son. When you get out, Ma and I will be right here waiting for you. If you've changed your ways by then, you're welcome back aboard and you'll always have a place on my crew. We just think this is the best thing for you right now. Tough love, as they say."

By about the second sentence in, his words had started to blend together into a meaningless porridge of patronizing gibberish. I bit my lip, shaking my head. "Dad, you and Ma should've stayed home. You never had it in you to sit by while your son took the reins of a ship you built yourself. I always got the feeling you regretted giving her to me. Someday soon, you'll regret taking her back."

I bent my will toward getting a reflex response, hoping the solenoid in my heel wouldn't make a fool of me again. A moment of awkward silence and two heartbeats later, it shot out like a dream and launched me off the deck. I soared over the bow and into a backward dive as the guns rang out, sending laser bolts and charged particles and hot shrapnel thrumming past my ears. I got hit twice, but I wouldn't realize it until later. In that moment, I was too busy falling.

# 2

ilfoyle's thugs had ripped a lot out of me, and not in a figurative sense. There were empty compartments all over my body where they'd eviscerated awesome, expensive tech I'd bought, begged, or stolen for. They'd reduced me to a shell of my former self by the time they tossed me into that hovercell. Now I was plummeting toward the Churn, its desolation spreading out below me in every direction, and I was still that same shell.

We'd been between drift-towns when the Civs stopped us, sort of a no-man's land where there were no platforms or large floaters. Now I found with startling certainty that there wasn't a single sign of life around, even as far as my telescopic eye could see. The nearflow was far below me yet, heavy gusts of wind carrying a field of airborne rubble over the surface.

You should know that driftmetal possesses a quality called *cumulative anti-gravitational mass*; that is to say, the bigger it is, the higher it floats. So the longer I fell without hitting anything, the lower my chances of hitting something big.

I clamped my eyes shut while I fumbled around in the pockets of the webgear I'd grabbed from the crew's quarters. I was playing the '*how-well-do-you-know-your-tech*' game show where the grand prize was not dying. I recognized each mod as my fingers felt their way along: flecker shield, tripwire, proxy remote, bluewave comm, scrambler, cochlear translator, muscle booster. No, no, and no.

Wait a minute. The first one.

With the sound of terminal velocity screaming in my ears, I ripped open the velcro fastener. I got a white-knuckled grip on the flecker shield and drew it from its pouch, opened the panel in my forearm, and shoved the mod inside. I tucked my body into a cannonball and flipped over so I was falling feet-first. I was plummeting at a frightening rate. When I opened my eyes, the nearflow wasn't so far away anymore.

A big floater caught me on the elbow and I cursed to myself. I would've cursed out loud, if the sheer terror of falling hadn't made my voice seize up like a clogged chimney. Soon I was pinballing off floaters the size of coffee tables and ironing boards, trying to grab hold of whatever I could, but failing. *You're going to make it*, I reassured myself, failing to reassure myself.

I waited until the floaters had decreased to the size of house cats before I bent my wrist back and activated the flecker shield. It wasn't a shield I needed, of course. What I needed was a parachute.

A metal rod shot two feet from my wrist and unfurled like a circular fan, a pleated metal ring designed to shrug off flecker particles. I raised it overhead like an umbrella. As I fell toward the nearflow, debris started to accumulate in the shield's underside. I felt myself begin to slow down.

The floaters were coming at me sideways now; the nearflow felt like being in front of a gigantic fan while someone was dumping out a bag of gravel. I managed to open one eye for a second and found myself closer to the ground than I'd imagined. The shield was helping, but it wasn't going to be enough to make the landing comfortable or painless.

I braced myself and hit hard, a bone-jarring impact I couldn't roll away from. I sank down to my armpits in loose Churn, my bare feet plunging through four feet of grit and gravel.

Yeah, it hurt like the dickens. Whatever the dickens are.

I ejected the shield and tossed it onto the surface beside me. All the bits of driftmetal and gravstone it had gathered began to float away. I yanked the bluewave comm from my webgear and flicked on the beacon, then tossed it onto the shield. The beacon would alert the Civs and bring them right to me, but I was starting to like the idea of prison better than the idea of suffocating in a sea of powdered stone.

The morning sun was just beginning to rise, but the air was so thick with dust and rubble down here that it was as dark as late afternoon. I felt a rumbling beneath me. Everything started to shake. My augmented eye went haywire, and my solenoid triggered.

A dozen yards away, the ground spewed a cloud of pink dust. I sank a little further. A rush of water choked up to my right and flowed down the side of a shallow hill before soaking into the ground again. I heard the rush of air as a pocket opened up behind me. There was a smell like eggs and rotting meat. Earth fell in and filled the pocket, and I slid a few feet backward.

I flailed my arms above me, trying to wiggle my way up a little and ease some of the pressure on my chest. This was a less active part of the Churn than the territory encompassed by

_J.C. Stewart_

Gilfoyle's mining operation. The land was coughing up dust and brown water and foul-smelling gases instead of quicksand and firespouts and boulders, so it could've been worse.

I felt another rumble, this time from somewhere in the distance. A pair of hoverbikes slipped over the hill where the dirty water had flowed up, moving fast through the dust haze. Their riders were hooded and masked, jacketed in long dark trenchers.

The first instinct I had was to fight. Anyone who made a habit of hanging out down here was, by default, savage, uncouth, and not to be trusted. Of course, when you can't trust your own parents, who can you trust?

I snapped the grapplewire mod into my forearm and tried to wiggle out far enough to snap off a clean shot. I didn't lead the hoverbike enough, and the wire flew wide of its target. The rider cranked something, and a tent of blue electrical arcs erupted around him, sucking the errant grappler toward itself like a magnet.

I tried to retract my wire, but the energy field had a better grip than my winch had pulling power. The biker hit another switch. Blue arcs bolted down the wire and zapped me rigid. My eyelight strobed, and my solenoid triggered three or four times.

When the shock ended, I went limp. I sank down to my neck. The gravel was pressing against my chest anew, the sour smell of electrical smoke in my nostrils and the taste of raw ozone on my tongue. My arms were poking up like broken antennae, and every movement I tried to make sent up new clouds of dust for me to breathe.

The bikers circled around behind me, and I heard them approach. Their hoverbikes were low to the ground, displacer engines thrashing the surface like leaf blowers over uncooked rice.

22

"What's a techsoul doing down here?" one said, yelling over the noise.

It became apparent to me then that these weren't just people. They were *human* people. Bona fide hundred-percenters, the kind without a scrap of synth in their bodies. As in, one step above Neanderthals.

I wasn't sure whether the guy was talking to me or to his friend, but in no uncertain terms, I told them both to mind their own business.

"That's an awfully rude thing to say, for a *tool* who's gotten himself into a bind like you have," said the other guy.

Humans call us '*tools*' to make themselves feel better about being the worst.

Since insulting them hadn't worked, I resorted to taunting them instead. "You guys seem to think you're pretty tough, picking on a defenseless techsoul when you know I could pound you into meat squares if this was a fair fight."

"Who said anything about fighting? You're the one who tried to start a fight with that grapplewire of yours," said the first one.

"Don't you try to bamboozle me with your technicalities. You should've seen yourselves, the way you looked from down here, zipping toward me a like a couple of fiery devils with hell's own fury farting out your tailpipes. Either you came over here to help me, or I'm going to keep thinking you came to pick a fight. Now which is it?"

"You have quite the knack for telling tall tales, don't you?"

I still couldn't see either of them, sitting behind me on their safe hoverbikes with the nearflow howling around us and the Churn belching below, threatening to eat me at any second.

"I don't have time to argue with a couple of *primies* about how tall my tales are," I said.

We call humans '*primies*' because they're extra the-worst.

"He's an uppity one," the first biker said. "Maybe we should just leave him here."

"I'll take my chances, if you're gonna be like that," I said.

"Have it your way," the other one muttered. He revved his hoverbike like he was getting ready to leave.

"Whatever cave you antiques crawled out of, I doubt it's any safer than this," I said, trying to sound as condescending as possible.

"Living down here isn't difficult as long as you've got the tech."

I scoffed. "Tech? Please. You primies wouldn't know tech if the Churn spit it onto your dinner plates."

"We've got plenty of tech. It's just not glued to our bodies like yours is. We found your bluewave beacon thanks to our tech. And by the way, some good your tech's doing you right now, blueblood."

"Hey. Up until yesterday I had a real slick kit. Some miner thugs pinched me and stole it all."

"Now why would mine workers do a thing like that?"

"'Cause they're lowlifes, is why," I said. "Now how about giving me a hand here?"

I've seen the Churn knock a streamboat out of the sky and swallow it whole. Trust me when I say I was at risk of being swallowed very, very whole.

"I'm sure you were just minding your own business when they decided to come along and mug you."

"They had pulsers. You tell me." I shrugged. My shrug gave the gravel a chance to crowd in and press harder against my lungs. All part of the master plan.

"Poor fella," said the first guy. "And how did you respond when these cruel security guards had their way with you?"

"I ate them."

As if in reply, the Churn ate me.

The ground opened and I fell fifty feet straight down until the bikers stopped laughing and decided to reactivate their energy field. I snapped to a halt, dangling from my wire like a rag doll. They hadn't stopped laughing, actually. I could still hear their whiny guffaws echoing down. I'd heard dying streambirds make nicer sounds.

The bikes began to rise. They dragged me with them, bumping and scraping against the sides of the pit as it collapsed in around me. I felt the gravel sucking at my legs just as I shot up above the surface. Good thing I wasn't wearing boots. The flecker shield and my bluewave comm were gone, devoured by the Churn.

"Where are you taking me?" I called up.

The grav engines were roaring and the nearflow was wailing so loud I don't think they heard me, but I saw why they'd been in such a hurry to leave. Captain Kupfer and his law-loving super troupe were coming down through the clouds, converging on the beacon's coordinates.

As much as these biker primies were pissing me off, it turned out they were also my heroes. They'd saved me from the Civs in the nick of time. *Fellow Civ-haters. We must be on the same team*, I realized. I couldn't tell whether the Civ Captain and his goons had spotted us, but I vowed that if I got away, it would be the first of many, many times I'd give Captain Kupfer a good screwing over. I'd get started on keeping that vow as soon as I got myself fixed up.

In the meantime, the primies were taking me back to their place. I get that a lot. Everyone I meet wants to take me back to their place. Usually to kill me. The primies' place was a drift-town like none I'd ever seen before. To be more specific, it wasn't a drift-town.

It was a *grav city*. And it was full of primies.

I could see the Churn hiccupping below as we passed through the cloaking field, a gigantic protective bubble that encased the city. My jaw dropped halfway to the Churn when I saw that the *entire city* was suspended on a gravstone bed. The land mass beneath it looked like any other drift-town, giant stone roots hanging off the bottom like a mountain flipped upside down, except that *it wasn't drifting*.

A network of polarized rods was holding it in place, about a quarter-mile above the surface. Neither the Churn's upheavals nor the brash, keening winds of the nearflow did anything to shift the city from its place. Even when they set me down on a shaggy carpet of grass in a lush green field, I felt no movement or tilt.

My first thought when I entered the city was to wonder if there were a hammer and chisel I'd overlooked in one of the pockets of my webgear. The amount of gravstone buried in the bedrock below this city was worth more than I could spend in a hundred lifetimes. The biker primies must've known there would be gold gleaming in my eyes, because they slapped a pair of steel wristbands on me as soon as we landed. I was resistant to the idea at first, until they offered to drop me back where they'd found me. Whenever I moved my hands more than about six inches apart, the magnets in the wristbands activated, snapping them back together with a painful *clack*. The device also gave me a nice little shock for my trouble.

The dome of crackling bluish-white energy above us looked a lot like the one the primie had generated from his hoverbike. Whenever a floater or a clod hit the dome, it glanced away as though it had struck a solid object, making almost no sound. I could feel a faint breeze and I knew the barrier was filtering the air, as clean and breathable as it was way up in the stream.

The two primies took off their masks and caught their breath. One had long, medium-brown hair and a beard; the other's hair was short, dark and curly, and he was clean-shaven. Both were younger than I was at the time, though I was better-looking than both of them put together.

"Muller Jakes," I said by way of introduction. I held out a hand and got my first dick-tickling shockwave of pain, complements of my wristbands.

They both laughed at me. The bearded wonder said, "I'm Clinton Vilaris, and this is Gareth Blaylocke."

"And this... is Pyras," Blaylocke said, waving a hand.

"Never heard of it," I said, still recovering. "You *live* here?"

Pyras looked sparkling-new, its sculpted white curves towering above gothic arches, like a scale replica of an ancient metropolis realized in styrofoam. Water cascaded down echelons of thick garden greenery, a maze of winding staircases and meandering walkways in smooth marble.

"You sound impressed," said Vilaris, scratching the beard. "Best part is, hardly anybody in the stream knows we're here."

*What the crap*, I thought, a little jealous. *This place is nicer than most drift-towns... and it's completely hidden?* After I was done thinking it, I said it.

"Not completely. We release the locks and move the city around from time to time. Just for safety's sake. It's not that nobody knows we exist. It's that we make ourselves hard to find."

My jaw was still hanging open. "How long?"

"Seven and a half inches," Blaylocke said.

Vilaris made a face at him. "Not likely." Then to me, he said, "A hundred and eighty-two years."

"You're kidding me. It looks brand-new."

I liked the thought of being somewhere the Civs couldn't find me. That thought alone made me want to stay a while. It was hard to believe there was a thing in the world the Civs hadn't gotten their grubby mitts all over. Being there gave me a sense of peace I hadn't felt in a long time. It was like having my own secret hideout and knowing it would last forever.

"We're standing on a magnetic island veined with several thousand tons of the most valuable element in the world, and you're doubting how we keep the place up?"

"I'm not doubting how you keep it up," I said. "I'm doubting how you keep it hidden. And why me? Why did you bring me in here and show me all this? I'm a few capers away from being the most wanted outlaw in the stream. I'd sell you out for a warm meal and a cot to sleep on right now."

"We have both, as it happens, and you don't have to sell anyone out to get them."

"Good, I'm starved."

They took me past blocks of the greenest landscaping I've ever stepped on, introduced me to a dozen other primies whose names I forgot seconds after hearing them, and brought me to a building they called the Kingsholme. Judging by the look of it, I assumed it was a cathedral or a library. Once we'd ascended the grand limestone steps and come through the towering entryway, an ornate affair of burnished brass inlaid with silver etchings, I found myself standing in an echoing stone hall with arched ceilings. A row of floating pedestals ran down either side of the room, displaying illuminated objects I could only assume held cultural significance to the city's residents. The pedestals were carved from dark stone marbled with exposed veins of driftmetal.

"This is great. Just, really great. Can we eat now?" I said.

Blaylocke was confused. "Wait. You eat food?"

"Are you dumb?" I said, incredulous. "What did you think, techsouls drank motor oil and ate roofing nails?"

The two primies shared a glance and burst out laughing.

"I swear, you guys..."

"Relax. We're messing with you," Vilaris said between chuckles. "Turns out you can't take a joke. I like that about you, though. It's more fun that way."

So I was a little uptight, being that I was suffering from a distinct lack of tech and my parents had just tried to serve me to the Civs on a silver platter. I wasn't feeling too good in the flesh department, either. I'd been shot, at least twice. Not to mention my whole body was gashed and bruised from falling thousands of feet through a cloud of floaters and landing in a section of Churn that was about as soft as a bathtub full of razorblades.

They led me down the hall and through the doors at the far end. A normal-sized hallway stretched from left to right. We veered left, then through a door, down another hall and past a large dining space furnished with a dozen pristine table settings. Through a swinging door with a circular plexiglass window, I was greeted by the sounds and smells of industrial cooking.

"Three bowls of gruel with a side of slop," Vilaris shouted.

The kitchen was a hurricane of white cotton twill and stainless steel, five in number. Their leader, a man as portly in stature as he was prodigious in toque, rapped the counter repeatedly with a metal ladle and shoved it in our direction. An underling obeyed, filling three bowls and carrying the tray past us into the dining room. Vilaris and Blaylocke followed him. I followed them. I was shoveling down spoonfuls of the tastiest gruel I'd had in days when the head chef came out to greet us, wiping chubby hands on an apron splotched with red-orange stains.

"Sheldon McLean, at your service," he said with a slight bow.

I stopped to cast him a sideways glance, then mumbled, "If you say so," between spoonfuls.

"I apologize for the slow service," said the chef.

Blaylocke waved away the apology. "Nonsense. You guys are strapped down tight in there. You should have a staff twice as big for the job you do."

Sheldon brightened, chins tightening beneath his five o'clock shadow. "We get by," he admitted with a certain note of pride. "How are things out there today?"

Vilaris shrugged. "Thick. Windy. Dangerous. The u'she."

I slurped the last dregs of my soup as though I were a condemned man enjoying his final meal, then let the bowl spin to rest on the table. To Sheldon's credit, he didn't bat an eye while the bowl *wub-wub-wubbed* to a halt.

"What is this place?" I asked, studying the ceilings.

"Kingsholme? It's the closest thing we have to a city hall. Pyras's center of arts and culture."

"So you guys can come in here and get free food whenever you want?"

Sheldon answered on their behalf, flashing a smile. "We're always happy to feed the City Watch and their friends."

"*Friends?*" I said. "I wouldn't go that far." I showed him my wristbands.

"It's a formality," Vilaris explained. "We're taking him to see the Innovators."

"News to me," I said.

"Maybe you should see a doctor as well," said the chef, no doubt having noticed my wounds.

"It looks worse than it is," I said. I tapped my synthetic eye with a fingernail. *Tink-tink.*

Sheldon's expression darkened. "Is he allowed in here?"

"We've reported it to the council already," Vilaris said. "There's a reason for all this."

"Ah." The chef gave a nod of sudden understanding. "My apologies. I didn't realize."

"Shel, ol' buddy," I said, "think nothing of it."

When you're a techsoul, you live without discrimination except in the presence of primies. Redbloods think they're better than you because they don't rust. They act like you don't both eat and crap the same. Blaylocke had had me there for a second with his little '*You eat food?*' ruse, but in truth he knew as little about what it meant to be a techsoul as all the other primies.

The chef took his leave after a moment of uncomfortable silence. Vilaris and Blaylocke thanked him for another fine meal. Sheldon insisted that it was hardly a meal and no trouble at all. Another series of hallways took us to a set of heavy wooden doors with riveted brass plating. The plaque on the wall read:

Department of Innovation
Prof. Dr. E. Chester Wheatley
Master Gadgeteer and Technotherapist-in-Chief

*Technotherapist?* I wondered. Vilaris magicked a steel key from his jacket and unlocked the door. The room beyond might as well have been in a basement for all its lack of windows, exposed brick walls lit by the orange warmth of coal furnaces and the cold white outbursts of blowtorches shedding sparks. I counted no fewer than ten men at work, each the picture of focus, armed with mallet and saw and rivet gun, encircling the skeletons of half-finished chassis like tribal hunters ganging up on big game. The workshop was a graveyard of gears, flywheels, pressure gauges, dynamos and pipes, all piled in corners, stacked on steel shelving units, and strewn about the floor.

Nobody noticed us. Vilaris had to send Blaylocke to fetch the guy whose name was on the plaque outside the door. What I'd expected to be some wizened old man was actually a guy about my age, a strapping youth bound in an exoskeleton of gleaming metal. A veil of black hair hung into his face, stringy-damp with sweat. When he removed his goggles they left wide pink circles in the skin around dark, tired eyes. I was smitten. If there was a man in this city who it could benefit me to befriend, this was that man.

"Gareth, Clint, good to see you. Chester Wheatley," he told me, thrusting out a greasy palm.

I took it in both of mine. "Muller, Muller Jakes," I said, shaking his whole arm vigorously. "What's this you're working on?"

He turned the upper half of his body to look, stiff-necked in his metal scaffolding. "Oh, that, just a new idea. My grandest idea yet. As they all are. Very secretive, you know. Everything we do here is very secretive."

*And yet we walked right in and no one batted an eye*, I almost said. His secret project looked to be something meant for flight—a light, winged frame about the size of a large dog, its internal mechanisms spinning.

"It's... magnificent," I said. "Really, I mean that."

Creases appeared in the skin around Chester's eyes. I like to think he would've stood a little taller if he'd had that much postural freedom. "You think so?"

"Without a doubt. Clean lines, efficient machinery, thoughtful design. You've really taken this to a whole new level. It's by far the most advanced model I've ever seen."

Chester was confused. "The most advanced... but this is my own design. Where could you have seen anything like it before?"

"Listen, Chaz. Walk with me." I would've put an arm around him if not for the wristbands. Instead I took him by the shoulders and guided him away from Vilaris and Blaylocke. "I know you work hard. I can tell you're a brilliant man. Lots of great ideas have taken shape here, haven't they? Yeah. This place is so full of dreams. So—" I paused for effect and panned my hands over the room, "—so... *pregnant*, with possibility. This is a place where dreams come alive. I can *smell* the inspiration." I could smell something, but inspiration wasn't it. "You have a gift," I said, looking him straight in the eye, "and you're wasting it."

There were wrinkles between Chester Wheatley's eyebrows. "But this... this flying machine will be the greatest invention the City Watch has ever seen. I've rigged up a bluewave communicator to send simple commands to it from a distance. Watch." He picked up a black plastic box that had once been an ordinary comm. Now it had a control wheel made from a copper gear, along with three extra buttons. When he turned the wheel, ailerons on the wings flapped in reverse of one another. "It's operable from as far away as the bluewave signal will go. This button will operate the built-in camera, after I install it. The City Watch will be able to fly it and take pictures of the outside without ever setting foot on the Churn. The Automaplane, I call it."

"This technology is *new* around here?" I acted incredulous. "Hate to break it to you, Chaz, but send me up to the stream with a few ounces of gravstone and I'll bring you back a fleet of these things. I'm sure I can find someone who still has a bunch of them lying around in their backyard."

Chester's bubble was burst. "Just when I think I've discovered something completely different," he said, the sparkle in his eyes turned to sorrow.

This guy got out of the house as seldom as I'd hoped. His Automaplane was a blasted brilliant idea. But I had places to go and things to steal. "Hey, don't get so down on yourself," I said. "You came up with this entire contraption without ever having known it existed before. If that isn't the mark of a true genius, I don't know what is. Chaz, buddy... others around here might not see your potential, but I do. You're one heck of an inventor, and if you don't see it in yourself, you need to be reminded." I reached through his scaffolding and poked him in the chest with both pointer fingers. "Your potential stretches further than you know. There are so many unexplored avenues of technology, the potential for finding that next big idea is right around the corner. Matter of fact, I think I may have already found it for you."

"Oh yeah?" he said, perking up. "What is it?"

"I'm a techsoul," I told him. "And I'd like to donate my body to science."

# 3

The neurological pathways that connect my body to its augments are nothing short of miraculous. Don't ask me why I was born with telerium-laced bones, skin the consistency of synthetic cloth, or bundles of polymer fibers for muscles. My veins are like fish tank tubing, my tendons and cartilage like hard rubber. Any given part of my body is twice as sturdy as a human's. Yet somehow it all works. I think and breathe and eat and crap and sleep like a human. Only I'm not human. Not as far as humans are concerned.

Even though I grew up the son of a mechanic, I've always felt like I've had an intimate knowledge of machinery in my blood. If something has moving parts, I can figure out how to fix it with the right tools. It's just hard to fix your own arm when the job takes two hands. So I'd offered myself to the study of E. Chester Wheatley not because I needed his expertise, but because I needed his hardware and a pair of skilled hands.

Techsouls are the unluckiest people in the world; we're also the most plentiful, by far. I've undergone more surgeries than I can count; most of the later ones I performed on myself. I've tried dozens of mechanisms to change the functions of my body and serve as convenient little diversions from having to think about who or what I am. When your body is part machine, you can't ignore technology. You can't *not* think about improving yourself and staying relevant. You wonder if anyone would take you seriously if you decided to say '*the heck with it*' and let yourself go, become an outdated model with rusty joints and toothless gears. Because the best thing about being human is never having to *literally* stretch yourself toward an ideal that says only the newest and shiniest tech is employable, only the latest and greatest is worth noticing. Primies are free from all that. They can lose weight or gain it, build muscle or pile on the fat, but that's the extent of the decisions they have to make about their bodies. It's possible for them to *understand* what it's like to be me, but they'll never *know*.

Vilaris and Blaylocke approached as Chaz—née E. Chester Wheatley—was opening up my various compartments to investigate my insides. My wounds from the fall were smarting something awful. I could tell I'd taken at least one flecker shot to the lower back and a laser in the butt, but I'd get those tended to later.

"You asked before why we decided to bring you into Pyras," Vilaris said. "We don't allow visitors often, but we need help."

I smirked. "I could've told you that."

"No, I mean we need *your* help."

"Sorry, I don't do the '*helping people*' thing." I air-quoted the words, keeping my wrists together like I was making a shadow puppet, while Chaz held a bundle of polymer fibers aside and peered into my thigh.

"This is unbelievable," Chaz was saying. "The way the synthetic flesh and the augments are so seamlessly blended together. I never thought I'd get such a hands-on view of a techsoul's body. The amalgamation of humanity and technology is astounding. This is going to change the course of my experiments for years to come. You have an array of neurosensors and twitch gyroelectrolyzers that are barely above detection, which I assume are intended for smoothing the interactions between the various brain-body-tech circuits. How does it all wire up, I wonder? How's it all connected? Oops. Did that hurt? How do you feel?"

"I feel close to either falling asleep or having an orgasm, depending on which one of those things you jab." I also felt weird having another guy's face six inches away from my crotch.

"If I tell you why we brought you here, will you at least consider helping us?" asked Vilaris, annoying me.

"Absolutely not," I said. "Unless there's chips in it for me, in which case I'd be working for you, not helping you."

"We can probably pay you a little for your trouble," Vilaris said.

"Well why didn't you say so? Or better yet, why didn't you just use the phrase '*work for us*' instead of '*help us*'?"

"Because you don't have a choice in the matter. We know you killed those miner thugs."

Chaz stopped fiddling with my leg. He shrank away, and I saw him gulp. "Killed?"

"It's not like it sounds, Chaz. They jumped me, and I—"

"Why are you lying?" said Blaylocke. "First our gravstone buyer ends his contract with the city. Then we hear the Civvies' chattering on the bluewave about so-and-so who's wanted for murder and attempted larceny. Then to top it all off, the Civvies come down into the nearflow and risk having their boats dashed to pieces to find said murderer. They were looking for you, Muller. You told us yourself you weren't far away from being the most wanted outlaw in the stream."

I gave Chaz a pleading look. "Chaz, I'm not a lunatic. You gotta believe me, I was minding my own business when—"

"Tell me the truth," Chaz said, shrugging out of his apparatus.

*Why do I have to be such a bigmouth?* "Okay, I stole something," I said, throwing up my bound hands. That made Chaz flinch. "I hid the haul on some floater and went to a tavern, planning to pick it up later in my boat. Gilfoyle and his goons found me first and said they'd kill me if I didn't show them where it was. I did, but Gilfoyle decided he wanted me dead anyway. They put me on a beat-up old hovercell and sent me to the Churn to die. If Gilfoyle isn't buying from you anymore, you should consider yourself lucky and find someone else to do business with. Someone who isn't a lying sack of crap."

"What did you steal?" Blaylocke asked, as though he already knew.

I hesitated. "Gravstone. A pretty big haul."

"And where do you think that gravstone came from?"

It hit me, and I knew where this was going. "At the time, I thought it was from the Churn mines. It wasn't though, was it? It was from Pyras."

Blaylocke shot me a look. "Do you know how we keep this old city so sparkling new? Why we're so wealthy even though we're humans? Because gravstone is our chief export. Every trade we make, every deal we strike, has to be done in secret. That's how we keep Pyras under the radar. In the case of our gravstone, it's by only dealing with one buyer. A buyer you tried to steal from. Who, after losing four of his men, a hovercell and a pair of hovertrucks, says it's too dangerous around here. He's packing up his operation and shipping off to friendlier nearflow, and he never paid a single chip for that entire truckload. That was almost half a year's output. You just scared off the only person keeping Pyras funded."

I'd ruined the economy of an entire city, and they wanted to pay me to fix it. I had to hand it to myself.

"We brought you back here because we want to give you the chance to make it right," Blaylocke continued. "Now that you know how many innocent people depend on the exports from our ore veins, you *must* feel some compulsion to help."

If I had said I felt one iota of compulsion, I'd have been lying. *They* were the morons basing their livelihood on the sale of a single element. Just because it was the most valuable element in existence didn't make it okay to put all their eggs in one basket. Besides, it's not like I had known I was screwing them over.

"So that's what you wanted to pay me for? You were going to throw some arbitrary number of chips at me and say 'Make it right'? 'Fix what you didn't know you broke'? What happens if I go out and tell the whole world about you instead?"

"Good luck finding us again, first of all," said Vilaris, running a hand through his long oily locks.

"And second of all," said Blaylocke, "that's going to be hard for you to do with the device Chester is about to install, which is the reason we brought you down here to the Department of Innovation."

"I'm doing *what,* now?" Chaz was so gullible and easygoing, I'd started to like the guy.

"Sorry for the short notice, Chester," Vilaris said.

"The old '*Do what we say, or we'll kill you*' routine, huh?" I said. "I expected better from you guys." I've always liked making people think I'm one step ahead of them. I also like being a wiseacre, so... two birds with one stone, there.

"Not quite," said Blaylocke. "We prefer to reward rather than punish. The device lets us keep tabs on you."

"A bluewave beacon? No thanks."

"It's not on the bluewave. It's a sub-signal. We're the only ones who can trace it. The device will let us listen in on everything you're saying. If we get wind of you doing anything that could jeopardize your task, you'll get a shock just like the ones from the magnetic cuffs and the cracklefields on our bikes. Keep it up, and we'll come find you."

"*That's* your idea of a reward?"

"The not-killing-you part was the reward."

"So I have no choice in the matter. You're forcing me to do this."

Blaylocke shrugged. "We were hoping it wouldn't come to that. We thought you'd want to help."

"Surprise, buttholes. I'm not a humanitarian. I don't work for free. How do you expect me to do this, anyway? Why don't you just do it yourselves?"

"We *will* do it ourselves, if you fail. But even as a wanted man, a techsoul can get around in the stream easier than a human could. You said you're an outlaw. Don't outlaws know how to sell things under the radar? When you stole all that gravstone, did you plan on selling it?"

"Sure," I said.

"To one person?"

I looked at him like I thought he was dumb. Wasn't hard, since I did. "Highly unlikely that I could've found one person who could afford all that gravstone. Probably would've had to find a dozen."

"So all you have to do is pretend you have enough gravstone to sell to a dozen people. Then find us those people."

"That could take months, if I'm lucky. I'd need a boat to haul it in, and a crew to protect it."

"As human as we may be, we do have brains," Vilaris said. "We're not gonna give you the gravstone in advance. That's how Gilfoyle burned us. You find the customers, we ship the goods."

"With the kinds of people I tend to deal with, asking them to take delivery after payment is as good as spitting in their faces," I said.

"There *is* one other option," said Blaylocke.

I waited.

"You could convince Mr. Gilfoyle to pay us back."

I laughed out loud. "The guy keeps a whole crew of thugs on retainer. If you think I'm ever getting within a mile of him by myself, you're delusional."

I wanted that medallion—the one I'd tried to trade away from Gilfoyle for his own truckful of gravstone. But I wasn't stupid enough to go near him again.

"What if you weren't by yourself?" Vilaris said.

"What does that mean?" I asked, leveling my gaze at him.

"Blaylocke and I will come with you. There isn't time to build a streamboat, but we can charter an airship from the city."

Blaylocke disagreed. "This is *his* problem, Clint. Let him figure it out."

"A crew of humans?" I said. "Please. Spare me the fairy tales. If anyone gets wind of me riding around with a bunch of primies, we'll all be dead before dinner."

"You're forgetting what kind of primies you'll be riding around with," Vilaris said.

"The kind with *cracklefields* and *magnetic cuffs*?" I said. "Ooh. The techsouls will be so scared, they'll forget to bring their skin augurs."

"You think we don't know how dangerous it is for us up there? That's why we want *you* to go," Blaylocke said.

"Yet you won't give me gravstone, money, a boat, or a half-decent crew. You'd better get ready to do a whole lot of crackling, because that's the only way you're getting me to move a muscle for your cause."

Vilaris gave a long sigh. "An airship and a crew of primies is the best we can do."

"Fine, but only if we switch from the airship to a streamboat once we get up there. I want to hire a few techsouls of my own choosing to supplement our crew. And I want Chaz to come. I'm gonna need a full kit and I'm gonna need it to be in working order."

Vilaris was too eager to wait for Chaz's response. "Sure, we can do all of it. And Chaz comes too."

"Deal," I said, quicker than quick. "Now will you take off these cuffs? I'm getting a headache from all the crackling."

Vilaris gestured, and Blaylocke obliged.

*Ladies and gents,* I thought, rubbing my abraded wrists, *that's how you turn incarceration into salvation.*

"Let's get moving," said Vilaris. "We've got lots to do and too little time to do it in."

"Chester, you'd better take the tool in for repairs," Blaylocke joked.

I snatched Blaylocke by the collar and lifted him, legs dangling. I could smell his breath, rotten from mouth-breathing and vegetable soup. "Don't *ever* call me a tool again."

I let him down, poked a finger into his face. "I will haunt your nightmares."

Vilaris had that look squirrels get before they decide to cross the street. I'd seen squirrels on Roathea, a floater that boasted both the largest city *and* one of the largest forested areas in the world.

"Get that crackler installed first thing, Chester," Vilaris said. "Will you be okay if we leave?"

I could tell Chaz was more afraid of me now than ever, but he nodded and stayed with me in the warehouse as the two City Watchmen left to find us a flight into the stream.

"I'm afraid my experience installing techsoul modifications is limited," Chaz said.

"That's okay, Chaz." He only flinched a little when I put a hand on his shoulder. "I wouldn't expect someone in a city full of primies to know how techsouls work. Fortunately for you, I know a lot about how I work. I have all the necessary ports and terminals. We just have to build some tech and make it fit."

Chaz gave an almost imperceptible nod.

"Don't worry, pal," I said. "I don't fly off the handle like that all the time. We can be buds without you worrying that I'm gonna flip out on you, right?"

"Sure," Chaz said.

I didn't believe him.

It took us a few days to gather all the junk we needed to start building. Before we'd so much as lit our first blowtorch in the effort, Vilaris and Blaylocke were already antsy to get going. Lots of pressure from the big guys, they said. A council of three ruled Pyras; two primies, and one techsoul who fancied himself a sort of primie-rights activist, allowed in the city only because he was celibate and he'd sworn off mods of any kind. They'd actually made him swear never to augment himself, so his living in Pyras was no temporary whim. All this and more I learned from Chaz, who had started to open up to me with a little goading and my repeated assurances that while I was no law-lover, I wasn't a psycho axe murderer either.

"Any chance I could meet this guy?" I asked Chaz one day while we were looking over a set of schematics I'd drawn up for the new-and-improved hydraulic legs I wanted.

"Councilor Yingler? He's a bit on the busy side, as I understand it. And he's forbidden to enter the Department of Innovation due to his Vow of Remaining."

"So I'll go see him in the council chamber. Where's that?"

Chaz didn't say anything for a while.

"Somewhere in the building, huh..."

He pursed his lips. "I shouldn't say. Blaylocke told me—"

"Blaylocke spews so much hot air he could get a second job as a furnace. Come on, Chaz, buddy. Introduce me."

"Before we leave the city, maybe," was all he said before he changed the subject.

An escort from the City Watch brought me home every night to the tiny apartment they'd made up for me. Another complement of guards stood outside my door all night, and a third brought me back to Kingsholme every morning. The city didn't like the idea of playing host to another techsoul any more than I liked being trapped there. They were serious about making sure I didn't find a way to seduce some primie woman and breed my way into their perfectly preserved gene pool. I got dirty looks whenever I went out in the streets, so I focused on designing a killer set of tech and spent all the time I could in the workshop with Chaz. It felt like imprisonment, but it sure beat rotting in some Regency prison.

My new kit wasn't the collection of sought-after tech I'd lost to Gilfoyle and his men, but when Chaz and I were done tinkering, I was satisfied. I felt confident again too, something I hadn't felt since the night they took it all away. And I was *heavy*, unused to being weighed down with so many extra components. If I'd wanted to shoulder a fuel tank the size of a cow, Chaz said, he could turn my feet into a pair of hover engines. Or if I wanted a turbine for a hat, he could make me a man-sized airplane. He had the idea of turning my fingertips into a swiss army knife, each one a different tool, and the one about putting driftmetal in my calves and rigging up a set of gravstone clinkers. He insisted that I install a few weapon mods until I told him any moron knows you never store explosives inside your body. If there's one thing a techsoul knows, it's how to exploit the tender spots on another techsoul. So I said 'no thanks' to all those things, but yes to a whole slew of others that I was planning to test before we got into the thick of things. As it turned out, I never got the chance.

On departure day, a sparse crowd had already gathered in the city square by the time we arrived to find a small airship waiting to bear us aloft. An envelope of thick canvas skin, the sausage-shaped gasbag was an unremarkable beige color. Rigging lines attached it to the boat beneath, an aerodynamic wooden craft as slender and graceful as an old seafaring vessel. Rotating prop engines were mounted to its sides, and it had a windowed command bridge at the fore.

"She's a beaut, isn't she?" Chaz said proudly. *"The Secant's Clarity."*

I hated airships. Slow, unwieldy things. *Like flying a turd on crutches*, Dad used to say. "You built her?"

"Designed, built, and flight-tested," said Chaz.

"How's she gonna hold up when we get rammed by a streamboat full of pirates?"

"You're the captain, not the gunner. You leave the ship's defenses to my more capable hands."

Chaz wasn't afraid of me anymore, and I wasn't sure I liked it. By the time the ship was loaded and ready to lift off, the streets were jammed with people. We stood on deck and looked out over the throngs, the four of us breakfasted and dressed in the finest trimmings Hildebrand's Haberdashery had to offer. *An entire city full of primies*, I thought. I still couldn't believe it. I basked in the attention, knowing I was a hot commodity. So what if half the city hated me and knew I was doing this against my will? The other half didn't. I couldn't help but observe the fairer sex amongst Pyras's citizens. *I don't care what anyone says—primie girls are just as gorgeous as techsoul women.* I decided not to share the thought with my companions, though.

I had the jitters, but they were a different kind of jitters than the heart-pounding, clammy-handed thrill of pulling off a big score. They were the jitters of knowing thousands of people were relying on me. Suddenly the whole thing stank of *helping people*. But what could I do? Chaz had installed that sub-signal shocker, bolted it into a compartment near my wrist that he'd locked with a cipher key. They could reduce me to a quaking pile of synth whenever they wanted. Blaylocke had convinced Chaz to let him hold onto the remote—even more reason to be on my worst behavior.

"You never did take me to see that techsoul councilor of yours," I said. "Think he'll show up for the big send-off?"

Chaz wrinkled his mouth. "Maybe."

"Councilor Yingler runs most of our errands to the stream," said Vilaris. "He's the one who used to trade directly with Gilfoyle. I don't think he'd like you very much. I think if he wanted to meet you, he'd have arranged it by now."

"Oh come on, everyone likes me," I said.

Blaylocke snorted.

"Everyone who's not an idiot," I said.

"You really think you're capable of finding us a crew?" Vilaris asked. "Reliable, honest techsouls?"

"Yes and no," I said. "Yes to the first question. No way to the second. You want *sailors* crewing this boat, or nannies? Reliability and honesty come second to skill and know-how."

"He can't do a thing," said Blaylocke. "We should've sent him on this fool's errand by himself."

"Yeah, well I'm *thrilled* about having you along, too," I said.

In the stream, hanging out with primies is like wearing a bathing suit to a wedding; you might as well ask to be ridiculed. Primies are nothing but Churn-scum to most techsouls. Some techsouls even hate primies so much they'll go out of their way to kill them, so the way I saw it, having three primies along didn't help my chances of staying out of trouble.

"I'll give you something to be thrilled about," said Blaylocke, patting the sub-signal remote in his pocket.

"I swear, Blaylocke, give me one more good reason to pop you in the jaw and I'll make sure you never carry another conversation without a paper and pencil."

We spoke to each other out of the corners of our mouths, all the while standing at the railing, smiling at the crowds and giving them the occasional wave or thumbs-up. Vilaris and Chaz had gotten used to my animosity toward Blaylocke over the previous weeks. I didn't like the guy, and I'm not the type to pretend I like you unless there's something in it for me. I couldn't put my finger on what I found so abrasive about him. I just knew I hated his face and everything that came out of it.

"Cool off, Muller," said Vilaris, eyeing me. "We're not even off the ground yet and you're antagonizing him already."

"I'm getting an early start," I said. "You gotta run laps before you can finish the marathon."

I wasn't sure where we'd find our future crew, of course. Most of the sailors I'd worked with were my father's men now. My poor *Ostelle* was on the Regency's payroll, commissioned to hunt thieves and wanted men like me.

We'd thought ahead in that regard. Chaz, Vilaris and Blaylocke had made themselves honorary techsouls at my behest, in secret from their friends and families. Techsouls and primies look alike until you get under the skin, so I'd shown the haberdasher how to make techsoul clothing. The pants had velcro panels in the inner thighs, the shirts and jackets had flaps that opened down the shoulders, and the boots had heel and toe ports. My companions were still human weaklings underneath it all, but at least they wouldn't stick out like ticks on an albino. As for rustling up a real crew—it was time to find out if I had any true friends left in this world.

# 4

Airships like *The Secant's Clarity* are nothing like streamboats. In a streamboat, the only way you'll ever fall out of the sky is if you lose your driftmetal runners. You're more likely to get an unwanted dose of 'up' than one of down. An airship, on the other hand, is just a big bubble. And bubbles can be popped.

In my capsule at the fore, I hunkered down over the controls of *The Secant's Clarity* as we rose toward Pyras's protective cloaking field. Through the wide glass panes that Chaz had assured me were unbreakable, I could see out from the belly of the beast in every direction but behind me. The crowds below were sending us a deafening farewell. Far above the nearflow's dark maelstrom, a pure blue sky awaited us.

Chaz had suggested we each take a section of the controls to divide up the work, but that could wait until we hit clearer skies. He'd designed the ship so a single person could control everything from one seat in case the need arose. Since my reflexes were faster, and since I didn't have the patience to shout out my orders and wait for them to be followed, I decided I'd shoulder the burden myself.

As soon as the topmost portions of our craft breached the dome, I began to feel the vibrations from the debris smacking the gasbag's envelope like fingers flicking a rubber balloon. *Did anyone in Pyras consider the implications of flying an airship through a hailstorm of magnetic stones, or is there somebody down there who* wants *us to fail?* Chaz didn't strike me as the type of guy who would've overlooked this in his design, but I supposed it was possible. The even more disconcerting thought was that if someone had planned to put us in an unsuitable ship as an act of sabotage, they were probably going to get away with it. Was that why Yingler hadn't wanted to meet me? *Quit being paranoid and fly the blasted thing*, I had to tell myself.

Wind hammered the *Clarity* and threw us into a tilt. The entire craft leaned so far sideways I could've waved to the crowds without bending at the waist. When I passed through the cloaking field, the roar of cheering voices went silent. All I could hear in its place was the nearflow's skirling. I could only imagine the peoples' cheers turning to gasps as the wind swept us up like a broom over a breadcrumb. I struggled for lift while the nearflow spit rocks at my windows. The air was as thick as dirt, my companions gathered around me and clinging to the girders like a pack of stranded rats. Vilaris and Blaylocke were grim-faced; Chaz was equal parts terror and nausea. It made me laugh. That was probably because I was all kitted out with new tech now. I didn't have as many reasons to be afraid as they did.

"You've got to take her higher," Chaz managed to shout above the din. "The exterior skin can only take so much punishment."

"I'll get us there," I yelled back. "Keep your crotch in your chair and let me fly."

I flicked my pedals and took us hard to port, letting the nearflow push us instead of trying to fight against it. I could've made a nice tight turn in a streamboat like my *Ostelle*, but the best I could do in this tub was wobble in a lazy arc as the stone-laden wind buffeted us. The windows sounded like they were about to burst, the constant *tap-tap-tap* of smaller rocks interrupted every now and then by the *whack* of a stone the size of a melon. I thought I was going to stomp the port-side turning pedal through the floorboards by the time we finally straightened out so the nearflow could wash us along in its tide. I turned the elevator wheel, watching the dials on my instruments quiver and spin.

"Watch your ballast gauges. We're flying too heavy," Chaz sputtered.

"Would you like to take over, or are you gonna shut up and let me drive?" I lifted my feet off the pedals and raised my arms into the air, like I was hanging from a set of stirrups.

"Drive," they all shouted.

I got back down on the controls, shaking my head and swearing to myself as the airship shuddered. *Buncha sissies*. I'd get us out of this—but as usual, I was going to do it my way. I hit the engines full speed and level, pushing us downwind. With the nearflow at our backs, the engines were getting blasted. I could hear the metallic clanging of the propeller blades slapping rocks aside. One sharp stone at just the right angle was all it would take before we'd find ourselves dealing with irreversible damage. Soon the ship began to falter and lag behind the speed I needed to reach to escape the nearflow. The torrent was so strong it was stunting the propellers' rotation.

Chaz's airship came with a few surprises, though. Surprises I'd had the foresight to ask him about previously. Now that we had some momentum, I cut the engines to prevent them from taking further damage. Then I opened the front ballonet valve, letting air out of the forward-most of the two internal sacs designed to act as counterweights. We nosed up while the wind pushed us forward. Soon we could see clear blue above us, and I twisted the rear ballonet valve open to level us out.

We had almost cleared the nearflow when there was a loud *snap*. The whole cabin shook and tilted forward. Anything that wasn't bolted in slid to the fore and clattered to rest in the window well. Chaz fell too, lost his seat as the cabin tilted vertical. He tumbled down head-first, slamming hard onto the glass. My heart skipped like a stone, boots slipping off the pedals as my weight shifted forward. Through the windows I could see in startling detail how high we'd risen. The airship's entire undercarriage was dangling from the balloon like a thumb pointing down from a fist, the nearflow pelting it even as the balloon itself ascended to cleaner air. Lucky the engines were cut, or they would've been pushing us downward.

"What the blazes do we do now, genius?" Blaylocke screamed, his ire directed at Chaz. Blaylocke was still in his chair, scrabbling for purchase and unused to his techsoul footwear. Vilaris had managed to climb around behind his chair and was clinging to the back of the seat.

Chaz didn't respond. Loose junk and a spatter of blood decorated the window below him. His unbreakable glass was the only barrier between himself and gravity. The rocks pinging the bottom of the hull were lessening in force now. The windows were caked with dust, obscuring the outside world in a dull brown film. The floor was sloping forward at around sixty degrees, I guessed. At least the ship was still rising.

I'd seen plenty of airships travel between drift-towns, but I'd never seen one take off from the surface and climb all the way through the nearflow and into the stream. There was one problem inherent in our current situation, which I was now coming to realize: there's no way to put eyes on what's above you when you've got a pudgy balloon in the way. Being the genius was Chaz's responsibility, not mine. So naturally, I beseeched him for advice.

"Chaz, you alright buddy? We need you. Stay with us, huh?" I called down loud and firm, clinging to my seat.

Chaz blinked. I hadn't noticed the awkward positioning of his body before he blinked. I heard him take in a deep breath. *Okay*, I told myself. *Time to put some of this fancy new tech to good use.* I spun halfway around and slid down to him, scraping to a halt on the retractable toe and wrist spikes he'd designed, leaving deep gouges in the deck.

"Chaz, ol' buddy," I said. "It's about time we found someplace to land. You with me?"

He looked up, groggy and half-awake. I was reaching toward him, my upper body anchored by one wrist spike, when the ship quaked. I heard something rasping along the canvas skin of our balloon, and I knew we must've run into the bottom of a big floater. The balloon was dragging us up the rocky underside. If it burst, we had seconds—seconds, before we dropped out of the sky.

Chaz took my hand. I hoisted him to his feet, my hydraulics hissing to afford me the strength. When the balloon cleared the edge of the floater, the undercarriage slammed against it and began to scrape up the side. The cabin's port-side wall disappeared in a storm of wooden splinters. Before I had time to do anything, another rigging line snapped. We tipped sideways, thrown toward the gaping hole in the side of our hull. Vilaris lost his feet and hung by his chair's armrest; Blaylocke's body whipped around, but he managed to keep a one-armed hold and found himself dangling above the chasm. Chaz slid into the corner window. I stayed where I was, anchored to my spikes like a fly on the wall.

We stuck. Some jut of rock snagged the hull somewhere, and we stuck there with the balloon above and the undercarriage dangling with us inside it. Through the splintered hull I could see the floater's rocky underside sloping away from us like the prow of a ship. Below us the nearflow blew the stones past in a dizzying sprint; below that, the Churn. Chaz propped himself up on his knees, subdued and too calm in light of the situation. Blood flowed from a wound in his head, dark and copious, matting his black hair to his scalp. Vilaris and Blaylocke had managed to gain some traction and were perched on the sides of their seats like frightened birds.

"Hang on," I told them, knowing how redundant a thing it was to say. *Let's find out how unbreakable this glass really is.*

It was a strange sensation, climbing a vertical floor toward the starboard side of the hull. When I got there, I gave the window pane a series of sharp strikes with my wrist spike. The blows left scratches; the glass trembled in its frame, but it held. I flexed my wrist. A steel dart about four inches long quivered in the wood beside the window. Again. Another dart sprouted beside the first. I drew one of Chaz's gravmines from a pocket in my webgear and rested it between the two darts. It was a squarish box the size of a child's building block. No explosive components, but a marvel of electromagnetic tech if ever there was one.

"Look sharp, fellas," I yelled down. I uprooted my climbing spikes and let myself slide down to Chaz again. "Sit tight, buddy. I'm gonna get you out. Promise."

The flecker wasn't a marksman's weapon; an approximation of aim was all I needed. I pointed straight up and fired. When the flecker particle skimmed over the gravmine, there was a familiar *clink*, like the sound of a streamboat's runners. The window pane blew off its frame and spun away in one piece. *Unbreakable, but not immovable.* The cabin shifted again. We were swinging away from the floater, loosed from whatever had snagged us.

I didn't waste time climbing. My grappler bit into the hull and took me upward. When I clambered out of the open window frame, we were beside the floater and rising. *I can jump that*, I told myself, doubting it was true. The longer I waited, the less true it would be.

I crouched and leaned into my jump, grapplewire trailing behind me through the air, breath caught in my throat at the sheer amount of open sky between me and the floater. At the pinnacle of that leap I knew I wasn't going to make it, so I locked the winch and jerked downward, knocking the hull sideways. I reeled myself up the deck, hoping I hadn't jarred any of my companions loose. On top of the hull again, I withdrew the grappler from the hull and took another leap. This time I shot my wire at the floater from above, latched on, and swung in below it, slamming against the underside.

The pain lanced through me, but I set the winch to reeling. *Maybe I should've let Chaz build me those hoverboots*, I thought, as I lifted myself onto solid ground. I wanted to lie there in the grass and catch my breath, let my body recover from the shock, but *The Secant's Clarity* was getting away. As soon as my grappler punched through the deck I let the wire slacken and ran across to the far side of the floater. I planted my feet there and staked myself in with a pair of shiny new solenoids.

A long, nerve-wracking few minutes later, I had reeled the *Clarity* to within reach. Vilaris and Blaylocke came tumbling out through the gash and helped me moor her down. I ventured inside and set the ballonets to refilling. Presently the wounded airship settled to rest, and we found ourselves alone in a sea of clouds, drifting along somewhere between the stream and the nearflow. I pulled Chaz outside with me and collapsed next to the two City Watchmen, who were hugging the ground as though they hadn't seen a patch of it in months.

"Well that was interesting, huh?" I nudged Chaz with my foot.

Chaz said nothing. Just smiled at me, a vacant smile with the corner of his mouth making a little upward twitch.

I sat up. "Chaz," I said. "You hit your head pretty hard. I need you to say something to me. Are you okay?"

Nothing. Just the same empty smile.

"Guys, Chaz ain't doing so well."

Vilaris lifted himself into a seated position. "Chester? Chester. Professor Doctor Elijah Chester Wheatley. Do you hear me?"

"Yes," said Chaz. "I hear you. Make me a tray on the seventh form of Kalican Heights with the gorge betwixt a jollity and his motes of singe-gutter. Can I hasten to gewgaw..." He stopped in his tracks, mouth hung open and staring. His jaw raised into another smile, something sinister in it.

Had it been anyone else, I would've seen fit to make a joke. But it was Chaz, sweet innocent Chaz, and for the first time in longer than I could remember, I felt guilty. I'd frightened him; tricked him. Shoot, I hadn't stopped *using* the guy since the moment I met him. He wouldn't have come on this little adventure if I hadn't insisted. Not that I was blaming myself. I never blame myself, even when I deserve to. Chaz was a brilliant man, with more potential in one breath than any dozen copies of Blaylocke. Yet here we were, stranded, with no way to get him the help he needed.

I exchanged a look with Vilaris. He was thinking all the same things I was.

"Blaylocke," I said, standing. "I want you to circle the ship and double-check all the mooring lines. The wind's picking up, and it's looking like we're gonna be here a while."

"Don't order me around," he said. "I'm the one with the crackler, remember? Why don't *you* check the lines while I sit here and have a rest?" He showed it to me, the gray plastic remote whose activation could turn me into a temporary colleague of Chaz's again. He was grinning.

I considered making a lunge for the remote, but Blaylocke was far enough away to press the button before I got there. "I was on my way inside to find a bandage for a buddy of mine who hit his head," I said. "But yeah, you just sit there and take a load off. And when *we* get off this floater, *you* can sit there on your keister as long as you want. What am I, your mom? Get on your feet and take some blasted responsibility for yourself."

I stormed inside, through the roughshod hole in the port side of our vessel. When I emerged with the medical supplies I'd found, Chaz was lying on his back in the grass. Vilaris and Blaylocke were crouched at one of the stakes near the ship.

"Come take a look at this," Vilaris said, motioning.

I stared at them, frowning in disbelief. "You guys left Chaz by himself."

"Because of this, yeah," said Blaylocke.

I ignored them and rushed to Chaz. He lay with his eyes wide open, staring up at the sky, midday sunlight painting him in shades of gold. The floater was no bigger than a skating rink, with room enough for the airship and a wide grassy border around it. There weren't many floaters this large so close to the surface. It was close enough to the nearflow that I could hear the winds howling if I listened. That meant the stream was much higher still, and we'd be lucky if we saw signs of life more than once every few days.

With his head wrapped in thick white gauze, Chaz looked like the refugee of some war zone. He had started to mumble to himself while I dressed his wound, his voice taking on a faint singsong quality at times. I wrapped the bandages around his head several more times than I needed to so the blood wouldn't show through, and left him to join the others only after I was satisfied the bleeding had stopped altogether.

"Bout time," Blaylocke said as I approached.

"Okay, what is it?"

"Look at this rigging line." Vilaris held up the end. "This is the first one that broke, while we were still in the nearflow. These ropes are thick. This is not the kind of thing that just snaps in half from a sharp rock in the wind. Look at the fraying around the edges. The breaking point is right in the middle, at the very top of the lift bag. Someone didn't want us making it out of there. Someone sabotaged the *Clarity*, and it's only thanks to you that we're still alive."

I ignored his thanks. I didn't have time to take recognition for good deeds done with selfish intentions. "Isn't Yingler the obvious choice?" I said. "Someone who secretly wants to oversee the downfall of Pyras so he can be the only living techsoul with access to all its wealth?"

"That sounds like a more fitting description of yourself," said Blaylocke. "*You're* the wild card—the stranger with a shady past and devious plans. Councilor Yingler has lived in Pyras for going on six years now."

I would've thrown Blaylocke off the edge then and there if I hadn't been so worried about Chaz wandering over it himself. Over my shoulder, he was still sitting in the grass where I'd left him. "You say '*six years*' like it's a long time," I said. "I've left *stains* I liked better than you more recently than six years ago."

"There's one major difference between you and Yingler," said Blaylocke. "Yingler is a trustworthy man. You're nothing but a petty criminal."

"Bloody right I am, and it takes one to know one, isn't that what they say? If you think a guy won't go to interminable lengths to hide himself in plain sight, or to paint himself as an altruist when he's really a scheming traitor, then your head is even further up your keister than I thought it was."

Blaylocke yanked the remote from his pocket and stood, backed away a few steps.

"Hide behind your little bug zapper again," I said. "What a brave man."

Blaylocke hit the button. A thousand needles pricked every inch of my skin, crawling over me like a swarm of metallic spiders. My whole body stiffened and I fell over, racked with pain. Solenoids and eyelights and wrist spikes flicked in and out, on and off. My vision was trembling, my body screwed up tight, a high-pitched whine ringing in my ears. I was erupting like some human alarm gone haywire. When the crackler stopped, I lay like a discarded toy, breathing.

"That's for emergency situations only, not just anytime you feel like torturing him," I heard Vilaris say.

Blaylocke's face blotted out the sky. "Just making sure it works," he said, amused.

I'd been all talk when they put the device in me. It was much worse than I remembered the wristbands being. Chaz knew the cipher, the way to open the seal around it. Addled as he was, I didn't see much hope in getting it out of him. It seemed the only way I'd ever be rid of this thing was if I underwent major surgery or took my arm off at the elbow. I could get a replacement, but those were expensive.

When I'd recovered some, I sat up on my elbows. "Don't fall asleep tonight," I said.

Blaylocke brandished the remote. "You want some more?"

"I want you to shut your yap and listen. Vilaris, you said Yingler was the guy who used to trade with Gilfoyle on the city's behalf. Why was that? Because he's a techsoul? Don't you find it a little strange that Gilfoyle decides to break your contract and relocate his mining operation, and then the Council sends *me* to fix the problem? That makes no sense, unless Yingler had a reason not to go fix it himself. If he knows Gilfoyle and he's on good terms with the guy, why wouldn't he at least make an effort? Does he *want* the city to go bankrupt? Because sending a group of expendables and sabotaging their mission seems like a good way to make sure it does. I'll bet you all the chips I have, Yingler and Gilfoyle were in league before I ever came into the picture. My theft didn't scare Gilfoyle off; it gave him the excuse he needed to leave. I think Gilfoyle and Yingler are conspiring against Pyras."

Vilaris was thoughtful.

Blaylocke was sneering at me. "That sounds like a convenient ploy to clear yourself of guilt," he said, "and it's a very convoluted way of arriving at a theory that isn't plausible. No one predicted you were going to fall into our lap like you did. Coming across your bluewave beacon in the Churn was a stroke of luck for us. Councilor Yingler is a shrewd man, and he saw that stroke of luck for what it was: an opportunity to fix what you'd broken without risking the lives of any of Pyras's citizens. That is, until you dragged us along with you. Now Chaz is half-dead and we're stuck on this rock 'til someone floats by."

"I've been working on airships all my life. I can get us airborne again, it's just going to take some time to flight-check all the systems. If I had Chaz to show me where all his tools are and give me a rundown of the schematics, it would be easier, but let's be honest—Chaz ain't exactly in a helpful mood." I checked over my shoulder again.

Chaz had gotten to his feet and was wandering around near the edge.

"Dangit, Chaz." I sprinted toward him and seized the back of his coat just as he was thrusting a foot out over the abyss. "Not that way, ol' buddy. Over here." I turned him around and walked him back to the ship.

"I guess we ought to chain him to the ground," said Blaylocke. "Anybody bring a dog collar?"

I was deciding whether to laugh or punch Blaylocke in the throat when Vilaris pointed. "Look, another floater. Just above those clouds, there. Something's built on it."

The small island was a few hundred feet higher than we were, riding a strong headwind. It was far enough behind us that I could just make out the shape of an ornate building beyond the parting clouds. My eye whirred as I zoomed in for a better look.

"Holy mother," said Blaylocke. "There's a symbol on the dome, there."

Vilaris was nodding. "Holy is right. It's a Skytemple of Leridote."

I grimaced. "Temples are for law-lovers," I said. "Screw law-lovers." Then I said something mean about law-lovers.

"Despite how you may feel, that temple is our best chance of getting help," said Vilaris. "Fixing the ship could take days. That's time we don't have if we want to catch up with that floater."

.C. Stoutt

"You still want to go through with this whole endeavor? Even if Yingler and Gilfoyle are in cahoots?"

"Even if they are, Pyras will starve without income. We produce our own crops and livestock, but there's plenty more we don't produce that the money from our gravstone buys. If Yingler wants us to fail, the best thing we can do is succeed."

"Fine. You're right," I said. "Just don't expect me to be pals with any of those Leri-dolts up there. Help me mend the rigging lines. We're gonna get the *Clarity* back in the air so we can chase down that temple."

2

# 5

Our little floater slipped away beneath us as I took the *Clarity* airborne. Wind whipped into the cabin through the yawning wound in our hull, filling the control capsule with cold, thin air. Vilaris and Blaylocke had strapped Chaz into his seat with a few lengths of rope to be sure he didn't fall or wiggle out while no one was watching. I felt bad about it, but something was wrong with the guy. We needed to get him to a place where he could get help.

It had taken us the better part of an hour to secure the lines and get the undercarriage balanced under the balloon again. In that time, the Skytemple had drifted past us and disappeared into the clouds overhead. I'd had to do some heavy convincing to get Blaylocke back on board. He was afraid the ship wouldn't make it more than a few feet off the floater. I was just as afraid as he was, only I wasn't a gutless wimp.

The prop engines sputtered to life, and I thanked myself in retrospect for shutting them off when I had. There hadn't been time to flight-check every last component, so I did a quick visual scan of my instruments to make sure there was pressure in the bag and clean air in the ballonets. I set the engines to slow speed and opened both valves. We lifted off, staying level. I didn't want to risk nosing up too steeply like I had in the nearflow. Too much pressure on any of the rigging could put us back in a similar predicament.

"There it is," Vilaris said, leaning forward in his seat. "The back of it is poking out through that cloud."

"Alright, I see it," I said. "Never thought I'd be in such a hurry to get to church."

Our little floater slipped out of view in the bottom windows. I pushed the engines to half speed, making sure I was rising faster than I was accelerating. We rose until we were at altitude with the Skytemple. I closed the ballonet valves and headed for the cluster of pillowy white clouds where our destination was hiding. Soon we were engulfed in a blinding cloak. I cut the engines to slow as wisps of cumulus licked the interior of the ship like white flames, dissipating in the crisp air of the cabin.

Something thudded against the hull.

"Not again," I sighed, thinking another line had snapped.

We came into clear sky, and the island temple spread out before us. It was a large floater, a tenth of a mile long at least, with dense forests and a mountain waterfall at its head. The temple foundations were of lavish gray stone, its wings and courtyards set on multi-layered terraces whose steps flowed over the contour of the land like rivers. There were towers and steeples topped by concave roof trusses, with porcelain shingles of a deep watery purple. Like most inhabited floaters, this one had a small airfield. There was a hover and two air barges, which the inhabitants must've used to transport goods and passengers.

The airfield wasn't large enough for a runway, but there were empty spaces for other ships to land. The whole thing looked welcoming enough, except that there were monks streaming out of doors and onto balconies, aiming crossbows and ballistae in our direction.

Vilaris swore.

"I *told* you I had a bad feeling about this," I said.

"No, you said you hated law-lovers," said Blaylocke.

"Was I wrong?"

Blaylocke didn't answer. Chaz was mumbling gibberish to himself.

"Well, I don't see any reason to stick around, do you? *The Clarity* is airworthy; that much we know. Might as well stay that way while we still can, or they'll turn this thing into a pincushion." I was twisting open both ballast valves and reversing the engines as I spoke.

We began to rise while crossbow bolts punched the hull, quivering. Others careened off the windows, while still more rose toward us and lost momentum before plummeting back down. The monks were dressed in purple robes that matched the color of the roofing tiles. They scurried around like ants, getting smaller and less menacing as we faded up and back into the clouds.

"Isn't Leridote supposed to be a peaceful god?" I said.

"Men have been fighting in the name of peaceful gods for as long as there've been gods," said Vilaris.

"They ought to know we didn't come here to continue the tradition," I said.

"Anything on the bluewave?" asked Vilaris. "Maybe you can tell them yourself."

I looked at the comm. "Not a thing. They didn't even send us a warning."

"Uh, are you watching this pressure gauge here?" Blaylocke asked, rising from his seat and tapping the glass.

The needle wiggled. The pressure in the balloon was dropping. I swore.

"Did we get hit in the bag?" asked Vilaris.

"Don't know what else it could be, unless a woodpecker got frisky with the ship while we weren't looking."

I opened the valves as wide as they could go and rotated the prop engines until they were vertical. We jerked upward, rising like a puff of smoke. I didn't care if we hit something; I was taking us as high as I could before we lost the ability to rise altogether. The pressure gauge was inching to the left, moving so slow it was hard to tell.

"We gotta find someplace to land this thing," Vilaris said. "I'm going above to take a look around."

"Send Blaylocke," I said. "I'm gonna need you down here in a minute."

A few seconds passed before I heard Blaylocke's spyglass *whisk* open and his boots clunk up the stairs.

"What do you need me for?" asked Vilaris. "It's not looking too good, is it?" He was shivering. Whether it was from cold or fear, I didn't know.

"No, it's not looking good," I admitted. "Good thing Chaz here is a prodigy. Ain't it, pal?"

When I glanced over my shoulder, Chaz gave me the response I expected: a warm, vacant smile.

"Find something sharp and start chopping up the floor. We're building a fire."

Vilaris frowned. "What?"

"We need wood. Make a pile and I'll tell you what to do next."

"I don't understand..." Vilaris was anxious, on the verge of breaking down.

I wanted to scream at him. I talked fast instead. "These ballast pipes vent through a furnace in the aft cabin of the ship. Build a fire, and the ballonets will fill with hot air instead of cold. It's gonna be a chore to fly this thing without ballast tanks, but at least we'll stay afloat if the main bag loses pressure. That enough of an explanation to get you moving?"

Vilaris sprang into action without another word. He snatched up the boarding axe hanging over the doorway and began hacking the planks to splinters. A moment later, Blaylocke stumbled down the steps into the cabin. He saw what Vilaris was doing and gave him a puzzled look.

"There's a floater up ahead," Blaylocke said, "about two o'clock. We're too far down and I can't see what's on it. We need to get higher."

"Doing the best I can," I said. "Help Vilaris with that firewood."

"Firewood?"

Vilaris filled him in with a five-second physics lesson.

I sized up the pile of wood he'd gathered. "Okay, that's plenty. There should be lots of unlit coal in the furnace room. Get a few shovelfuls in there and burn what you can. The wood will start faster and burn quicker until the coals get going. Now move it."

The two men left the command capsule with their arms full of firewood, leaving me to coax every inch of altitude I could get from the *Clarity* before it turned to stone. The needle on the pressure gauge was still sinking. Even with the prop engines pushing us vertical, we were creeping upward at a disheartening pace. Chaz was speaking softly to himself, still tied to his chair. I leaned forward to catch a glimpse of the floater Blaylocke had mentioned, but all I could see past the balloon's bulk were clouds and the open blue of the sky. There were folds and creases inching across the balloon's surface, visible signs of the loss in pressure.

*I should've told them to let me know when they got the furnace going,* I realized. "How you doing, buddy?" I said, giving Chaz a smile.

He didn't smile back this time. His brow wrinkled. He licked his lips. "I... I don't... know," he said.

"Chaz? Chaz. It's me, Mull. Do you understand me?"

Silence, and another confused look.

"Chester," I said. "Chester Wheatley. Is that your name?"

Chaz sighed. His head lolled to one side. He blinked, raised his eyebrows, closed his eyes as if enduring a bad headache. "Without a doubt."

"Chester," I repeated, turning to face forward again. "If you can understand what I'm saying, I need you to talk to me. It's very important."

"What..." he said, trailing off into another sigh.

I wanted to go to him, but I didn't dare leave the pilot's seat now. "You're tied to your chair. Can you find the knots and start untying yourself?"

Another moment of silence. "I can't... move my fingers. It feels stiff when I... try to tell my hands what to do."

"Just a little hiccup in the fine motor skills, pal. Keep trying. You took a hard hit to the dome, but your brain knows what to do. Concentrate."

The needle on the pressure gauge fell into the red. I pushed the engines past half speed and up to full. The altimeter stopped rising, started falling. So did we. My stomach leapt into my throat, a rush of fear and adrenaline. We were sinking, a slow and continuous descent. All the upward thrust *The Secant's Clarity* could muster couldn't prevent us from falling anymore. *Dangit*

*Leridote, if we have to land on that Skytemple of yours, I'm gonna be pissed...*

Vilaris came leaping down the steps, hoisting himself by the handrails. "We got the fire going. The air's warming up, but it's not hot enough yet."

"How much longer?" I asked.

"Another minute or two."

I bounced my knees, drummed on the armrests with my fingers; reached for the valves, took my hands away. "Untie Chaz," I said after a moment. "He's doing better. I think he understands it when you talk to him now."

Vilaris obeyed. "Chester? Do you know who I am?"

Chaz cleared his throat, gulped. "Yes... I can remember. I know you."

"What do you think?" I interrupted, feeling the ballast pipes for warmth. "Now?"

"I don't know. Try it," said Vilaris.

"I can't *try* it. If I fill the ballonets before there's hot air in the pipes, they'll fill with cold air instead and we'll drop even faster. Here, take the helm for a minute. I'm gonna go check."

I leapt over the controls and darted up the steps, taking them two at a time. On the deck, the clouds were rushing by, heading upward too fast now for comfort. I descended into the aft cabin, where Blaylocke sat tending the fire. His face had a dour look, black smudges and fingerprints across his eyes and nose.

"How's it looking?" I asked, crouching to get a look at the furnace myself.

"Fine." He was listless, his face a mask of sorrow.

I felt the exhaust pipe and the lines that snaked across the ceiling toward the command capsule. Both were hot to the touch.

"We're going to be alright. Just keep that fire going, and keep it as hot as you can."

Blaylocke nodded, staring into the flames as though he hadn't heard me.

"What's the deal with Blaylocke?" I asked Vilaris when I'd returned to the controls. I was already cranking the valves to start the ballonets filling.

Vilaris gave me a knowing glance. "Is he still looking miserable back there? We couldn't find kindling to start the fire with, so Gareth had to use parchment paper... including a letter he'd written to his wife. When we started falling, he got pretty upset. He was like, '*We won't survive this time. This is it. It's the end.*'"

"How was he planning to mail letters to a hidden city that nobody knows about?"

"He was going to write to her every day, like a journal of sorts, and give her the letters when we got back."

I shut my mouth. I didn't know what it was like having a family you *wanted* to get back to. Not anymore. I'd only been away from my parents for a few weeks, but I could say without reservation that they'd been the best few weeks of my life—torture and other hardships aside. Being on your own was the absolute *nuts*, as far as I was concerned. I didn't need anyone, I told myself, unless they had the potential to be of use to me. Blaylocke was weak, and that gave me another reason not to like him.

Soon we stopped sinking and leveled out. After a minute, the ballonets filled up with the warm smoky air from our impromptu fire, and we began to rise again. I rotated the engines to push us forward, knowing I'd have to use engine thrust alone to control our altitude now. We collided with a thick head of clouds and found ourselves engulfed in a pocket of obscuring mist. I sent *The Secant's Clarity* rising faster, wanting to escape the feeling of sightlessness before anything else went wrong.

When we cleared the tops of the clouds, they became a carpet below our feet. The airship seemed nothing more than an insect, soaring over the soft white blooms of a cotton field. Grand, stately floaters drifted on skyward currents, massive islands replete with sprawling towns and palatial cities that dotted the blue as far as we could see. Against all odds, we'd reached the stream.

I felt a heavy hand on my shoulder. It was Chaz, standing behind me, unsteady on his feet. Vilaris was supporting him on the other side. There were tears in his eyes. "I never imagined it could look like this."

"Yeah, it's pretty great, isn't it," I said.

"It's a whole 'nother world."

"Looks can be deceiving," I said. "Especially for you guys."

Vilaris was in a similar state, his eyes wide and shining with the reflection of the sky. "So... what do we do now?"

"We pick one."

We let Chaz pick. He chose the closest, easiest landing spot, a massive floater I recognized as Mallentis, home to the twin cities Hibantya and Eulaya. Each city sat high up on its own plateau, the two joined together by a series of colossal steel bridges that spanned the canyon running between them. We got bluewave clearance from the crow's nest and touched down in the wide valley that ran out from the canyon like a river delta, a grassy field strewn with airships.

Travelers too poor to afford accommodations in the cities were camped out at their ships, chatting and carrying on like the attendees of some big peace festival for land-huggers. Multi-bagged helium dirigibles sat beside sleek hoverships and small, lightbulb-shaped hot air balloons with brightly-colored skins.

There were sleek streamboats of every size, copters and prop planes, and even a few gliders. *The Secant's Clarity* looked like a greasy rag in a sea of silk robes, its hull sundered, its plain envelope sagging over the two ballonets within.

"Someone should stay with the ship," I suggested, after we'd secured the mooring lines and located the hole where the crossbow quarrel had pierced the skin of the balloon.

"I'll go with you," said Vilaris. "Gareth and Chester should stay here and get some rest. Stay on the bluewave, Gareth. And be sure to listen in on Muller's sub-signal, too."

Neither of the men objected, so Vilaris and I made our way toward the canyon as the afternoon shadows lengthened on the cliffs. A set of elevators ran up each side, bullets of gleaming brass rocketing hundreds of feet through open shafts lined with pulsing blue lights. The elevators on the left took passengers to Hibantya; the ones on the right, to Eulaya.

"Which way?" asked Vilaris.

"Depends. You want to buy a streamboat or rent one?"

"What's the difference, price-wise?"

"That's like asking how much food costs. How much of it do you want? What kind? Do you want to wash your own dishes? There's no simple answer unless you can be more specific."

"We charter a fifty-foot ship, complete with captain and crew. Or we buy that same ship and hire each crewmember separately. How much of a difference are we talking?"

"Okay... roughly? About a year's salary. Now, if it takes us longer than a week or two to find Gilfoyle, your rental costs go up. And this is all assuming we don't let slip that you three are... who you are. It costs extra to keep mouths quiet, you know."

"Right. So you know some people? Some sailors, I mean? What do you recommend?"

"I say we go both ways. That sounds bad—let me explain. Eulaya is where the rich folks live. The smaller of the two cities, the less crowded, and the more exclusive. Anybody who owns a streamboat worth buying will be there. Once we have our boat, we cross over to Hibantya and round up a crew of the most despicable, cutthroat sailors we can find. And we put an ear to the ground for information about Gilfoyle's whereabouts while we're at it."

We veered to the right at the edge of the airfield, where a handful of gypsies was dancing around a raging pit fire, while a dozen more sat in the shadows of their airships looking on.

Vilaris gave the gypsies a wide berth. "I hope you don't plan on hiring anyone too despicable. No... pirates, or anything."

I scoffed. "Pirates. What *is* a pirate, really? You've never stolen anything in your life? *You* might be a pirate, for all I know."

"If having stolen something were the only criterion, most people would be pirates. You, especially."

"I beg your pardon," I said. "I prefer to think of myself as a commodities appropriation and merchandising specialist."

"Isn't that the same thing?"

I shook my head. "Pirates steal for glory and adventure. I steal for no reason at all, and regardless of whether it's necessary."

Vilaris rolled his eyes.

We approached the elevators that would take us up to Eulaya. A squad of green-clad customs officers stood by, processing the tourists, merchants, and cargo shipments that were coming and going. The narrow canyon was filled with them; crowds of people and their wagons and carts carrying all manner of trade goods and supplies. We waited in what passed for a line while the sun began to throw rays of pink and orange across the clouds. Soon one of the officers, a tall thin man in a stiff green suit, stepped toward us with a clipboard and pen in his hands.

"Welcome to Mallentis, gentlemen," said the man. "Are you citizens or visitors?"

"We're all citizens of the world, aren't we, my good man," I said. "Say, how tall are these cliffs, here?"

"On this side, close to three-hundred feet. On the Hibantya side, a little over two-hundred. Now—"

"The easier for the haves to look down on the have-nots, eh? Which side do you live on? You're a Hibantyan, I'll bet."

"That's right. Now, sir, I need—"

"I knew it. A man of the people. I figured on that the second I saw you. What's your name, old chap?"

"Andrew Partridge," was all I gave the officer time to say.

"Andrew... Hal Nordstrom." I took Andrew's clipboard and shook the hand that had been holding it. "Pleased to meet you. Heavens bless men like you, who work so hard to keep this place organized and on the level for the upstanding businessmen of the world. Thank you so *very* much for your service. Say, we're in need of a little help. Would you be so kind?"

"Certainly, but first—"

I handed him the clipboard without stopping to take a breath. "We'll be wanting a quick bite and some rousing conversation. Do you know a place that can offer us both? Cost is no object. My friend here is a moneyed man." I prodded Vilaris with an elbow. "Not a working stiff like you and me. Truth be told, I can't stand the fellow. Wretched man. Wouldn't know a hard day's work if it slapped him in the face. Look at him. Can't you see it in the way he carries himself? He puts on airs, what with the shaggy beard and unwashed appearance. And yet, do you see how new these clothes are? Exactly the way a wealthy man *would* disguise himself. Any suggestions for a lively place where this deplorable creature and I might dine this evening, Andrew, old friend?"

"There's the Crescent Restaurant, The Hart's Antlers, and the Cliffline Resort. Those are where I'd go if money were no object. But sir, please—"

"That's very kind of you, Andrew. Now don't misjudge me: I myself am guilty of having come into a little extra coin every now and then, but every chip of it is thanks to a generous helping of hard, honest work. If we weren't only passing through for the night to pick up a few supplies for the voyage home, and you weren't otherwise engaged, I'd offer to take you with us in thanks for your dedication to the safety of Mallentis. That'll have to wait for next time, however. We'll be sure to call on you when we're in town again. You can show us the sights, and we'll show you a good time. How does that sound?" I turned to Vilaris. "Be sure to give Andrew here a generous tip, will you, you wealthy son of a gun?"

I began to move past Andrew toward the elevators. He had been scribbling on his clipboard as I talked.

"Uh, sir... Hal. Mr. Nordstrom," said Andrew, following me. "Where did you say home was?"

I hesitated. "Bannock. Little island that keeps a low altitude, a distance downstream from here."

"Ah, yes. I know the place," Andrew said, scribbling.

"You've been there?" I said with excitement. "Oh, splendid. Quaint little drift-town, Bannock, isn't it? Lovely all the time." When I turned around, Vilaris was giving me his dirtiest look yet as he dug a hand into his pocket.

"No, I've never been," said Andrew. "I only know it by name. And what do you do for a living there in Bannock, Mr. Nordstrom?"

"I'm in the business of moving things from one place to another, Andrew, my boy. I take them where they need to go, and the people who own them reward me for having done so. Tell you more about it next time, 'ey ol' buddy? Now, will you still be down here about three hours from now?"

"My shift ends at eight o'clock," said Andrew.

"Very good," I said. "We might even run into one another again before the day's out."

"We may well," said Andrew. "Now if you please, may I have this gentleman's name and information as well?"

"Lincoln Putch," I said. "One of my investors. Terrible fellow, really. If I were you, I'd lock him up for no other reason than the dour looks he'll give a man from time to time. See, there's one of them now. Good thing these decisions aren't up to me, I dare say. Best leave that to the professionals, eh? For you and your like, Andrew, there is no end to my admiration."

Vilaris handed Andrew a small fold of chips, which he accepted with a nod of thanks.

"Now then," I said. "Which elevator is ours?"

Andrew smiled. "Right this way, Mr. Nordstrom."

When the doors slid shut and the ground began to pull away from us, a wave of relief washed over me. *We made it into the city*, I thought. *Next comes the hard part.* The blue lights flitted by as we shot upward, reflected in the elevator's plate glass windows. Spots of yellow-orange flame smoldered in the valley below, torches and campfires underscored by the growing dusk. The airships that had been so large when we stood next to them became no larger than toys; the people, no larger than bugs. Vilaris and I were alone in a box of glass and metal large enough for twenty people.

"What was that all about?" he asked.

"I was just being honest. You *are* a wealthy son of a gun."

"No, I mean all that nonsense about why we're here."

"Did you want him asking detailed questions about what we're *really* doing?"

"What does it matter? We're finding a streamboat and a crew. That's not illegal."

"Okay, so three primies from a secret city are here to find a ship and fill it with sailors, steal back the gravstone their former business associate walked away with, sign trade contracts with a dozen new buyers—trade contracts for the most valuable element in the world, mind you—and return home without leaving behind a trace of their existence. Is that what you wanted me to say?"

"I didn't say that. But you didn't have to embellish your story so much."

"Let me tell you something, Clint. Those customs officers aren't just there to make sure everyone's following the rules. They're there for a piece of any good action they manage to uncover. You think they don't take bribes? Think they don't report suspicious activity at the drop of a hat? It doesn't matter if we're breaking zero laws or a hundred of them; they can throw you in the hothouse because they don't like the way you smell."

Vilaris tossed up a hand, defeated. "Alright. What do I know? It was a little over the top, that's all I'm saying. But I guess it worked."

The elevator halted a few stories from the top of the cliffs, and the operators cranked the doors open. Instead of the city, we stepped out into a damp gray cave with harsh white bulbs flickering along the ceiling. Four customs officers in dark green uniforms were standing on the other side of the doors as if they'd been waiting for us, solemn and stern-faced, golden badges glinting in the cold light.

"Just this way, please," said the first of them, a broad-shouldered man with a shock of blond hair showing beneath his crisp green cover.

Vilaris and I followed. The other officers didn't move until after we'd passed them. I noted their sidearms, black snub-nosed revolvers, probably loaded with pulser rounds. The floor of the cave was smooth and flat, the walls rough and curvaceous. They led us down the arched hallway and we turned right into a side corridor. When two more officers appeared outside the doorway of the small windowless room ahead of us, I knew something was wrong. I'd guessed it as soon as we left the elevator, but now I knew. I kept up the act nonetheless.

"Eh, excuse me, officer. We're meant to be headed into the city. Where are you taking us, exactly?"

Heedless of my words, the officer swept an arm toward the doorway. "Just through here, gentlemen."

I stopped in my tracks. "Excuse me, I said. I demand to be told where you're taking us."

I heard hands brush against holsters behind me.

"Mulroney Jakes, we're placing you under arrest. You're to remain here until the authorities arrive."

*Andrew Partridge, you sly rascal. Sold us down the river without a hint of betrayal in your eyes, and I didn't even catch on. Heavens forbid I ever come back to town to find you...* "That won't be necessary," I said. "I'm turning myself in."

# 6

I stuck my hands in the air and turned to face Vilaris. "Elevator. Run."

Vilaris was confused. "Huh?"

I didn't have time to spell it out for him. I shoved him aside and put a dart into each of the three officers' chests before they'd unsnapped their holster straps. Without turning around, I pulled my flecker pistol from inside my jacket and shot the blond-haired officer in his big meaty head. "Run. Dangit Vilaris, run!"

The two officers in the doorway had drawn and started firing before Vilaris and I were halfway down the side corridor. I watched the pulser rounds explode around Vilaris and make the hair stand up on the back of his neck, but he managed to avoid taking any direct hits. Not that pulser rounds would've had much effect on primie flesh.

When the first pulser round hit *me*, on the other hand, it felt like someone had wrapped me in electrical wire and stuck me in a toaster. My bones lit up like fluorescent bulbs, and my skin crawled with those little robotic spiders that have sewing needles for legs. Two more rounds hit me while I was still in the process of collapsing, igniting my body in their electromagnetic agony.

Vilaris heard me fall and came back. He came back for me. Lifted me, dragged me to my feet and carried me, firing flecker rounds over his shoulder while we charged down the hallway. Someone hit the alarm as we rounded the corner. A siren wailed, loud and long and keening. The elevator lay ahead, our gate to freedom.

I hurt. All over. It's just like the cops to put you in the worst possible pain you could be in without doing any real damage. I'd been hit with pulsers before, mind you. The miner's thugs had used them on me earlier in the same night I escaped from the hovercell. That hadn't been my first time getting pulsed, but gouge my eye out with a rusty fork if it hadn't hurt more than the time before.

It was the worst feeling in the world, getting pulsed. Worse than getting crackled. It felt like your body was in the process of being melted down for scrap. Knowing you'd be back to normal in an hour or two didn't make it any better. At least a flecker knew how to sear the flesh off your bones. At least a laser could burn a real hole in you. A pulser was little more than a hallucination of pain—the most powerful hallucination I'd ever undergone, including the ones I'd undergone by choice.

"Hold on, Mull. Not too much farther," Vilaris was saying.

Somehow my augmented eye had zoomed itself all the way in, and my unenhanced eye was trembling like a coin on a train track. Trying to see anything felt approximately as effective as using a snow globe to look through a kaleidoscope with the lights out. The sound of footsteps echoed around us, and Vilaris was dragging me into the elevator and trying to figure out how to get us to the bottom. I leaned into the glass, my head swimming and my legs wobbling like jelly. The doors slipped shut as customs officers raced down the hall after us. Then we were descending, and I was putting my back to the window and reaching for Vilaris.

"I promise that after tonight, I will try not to ask you to do this ever again," I said. "Hug me."

Vilaris gave me his usual look of bewilderment.

"Come here and wrap those big sexy arms around me, Vilaris, curse you. I don't have time for your games." I leaned hard against the window and planted the bottom of my foot against the glass.

Vilaris took a step toward me.

I yanked him in close, whispered in his ear. "Pretend it didn't happen this way."

My heel port *snicked* open. The solenoid jackhammered the window, and an instant later we were floating downward on a bed of crystalline shards. I felt the grappler chomp into the elevator ceiling and let the winch loose, Vilaris's startled screams and desperate, scrabbling arms worrying over my pained body.

He held on, heavens help him. Held on until I squeezed the winch tight and set us down like a couple of butterflies landing on a flower. Butterflies with rocks strapped to their ankles, landing on a flower made of the ground.

The winch was screeching inside my arm by the time we slammed down. Friction smoke was pouring from the wrist port as I ejected the wire and freed myself from Vilaris's bear hug. I could hear the alarm ringing faintly through the open elevator shaft far above.

A group of customs officers came toward us. Vilaris pulled me into the crowd. Whatever they called those tunnels and dark rooms where they brought people who didn't pass muster, neither of us wanted to wait around and find out. We were shuffling through a crush of bodies, ducking around baggage trains and pallets of building materials and carts full of wilting produce. Then we were in the airfield, darting through the maze of ships and campsites. My legs still felt like jelly and my head was pounding. It was only Vilaris's constant guidance that got me back to *The Secant's Clarity* without curling up into the fetal position and crying alone in the dark.

"No way we're going up in this thing again," I said as we entered the control capsule through the gash in the *Clarity*'s hull. "We have to find another ship."

"That's what we just got back from failing to do, isn't it?"

I draped myself over the pilot's chair, my body still throbbing like a sore thumb. "What we *tried* to do was buy a streamboat in good condition from a rich person who took good care of it. What we're down to now is finding any ship that flies, and getting off Mallentis before the cops find us."

"I'll start looking." Vilaris moved toward the exit, but I stopped him.

"Where are Chaz and Blaylocke?"

"Crew cabin, maybe? Or aft, keeping the furnace going?"

"Never mind," I said. "You go. I'll find them, as soon as I can stand up without my knees clacking together like cold teeth."

I sat alone, watching traces of firelight dance on the window panes, a cool nighttime breeze blowing in through the gash. My legs were splayed out, my arms hanging over the armrests, my back and neck both as stiff as a winter frost. No position I tried sitting in was comfortable.

After a little while, I stood and stretched. It felt like my whole body had a headache. A veil of malaise descended over me as I passed through the cabins in search of Chaz and Blaylocke. I found them both sound asleep in the crew cabin. The remote that controlled my sub-signal crackler had slipped from Blaylocke's dangling hand and was resting on the ground next to his bunk. I snatched it up without a second's hesitation and shoved it into my pocket.

I was free. It took me a moment to come to grips with it. I had the remote; it was mine now, and I could walk away. I could abandon this *fool's errand*—Blaylocke's words, not mine—and return to was important: getting my *Ostelle* back. Getting revenge on the parents who'd sold me to the Civs.

Once I had my boat back, I'd throw every last one of those stinking traitors overboard. I could already feel the smooth spokes of her wheel in my hands, feel her deck tremble beneath my feet as the turbines thundered. I could see her skimming across the sky, cutting a knife-line path along a misty yellow morning. I wanted to be there, walking through the clouds. I wanted to shut off the engines and let her glide, let the stream carry us away to anywhere.

*No more thinking about it,* I told myself. *I'm going.*

I moved for the door, but when I got there, I found I couldn't go any further. It wasn't because there was some force field blocking me. Not a physical one, anyway. It was because somewhere, down in the dirty black depths of my soul, a hint of morality was piercing the darkness like an ooey-gooey, compassionate beam of light. *If I leave, I'll be putting an entire city full of people in jeopardy. A city that might be the only true lasting remnant of the species I evolved from. Humans—humans like they were meant to be.*

In that moment, everything in me wanted to leave those stupid primies behind and never look back. Everything, that is, except the one tiny part of me that knew I couldn't. Curse that part of me.

"Time to get up, fellas," I said. "Wakey, wakey. We gotta get off this floater before we're knee-deep in law-lovers."

Blaylocke jolted awake; Chaz shifted in his bunk and opened his eyes. The two men looked at me with bleary, uncomprehending expressions. It was dark in the cabin, so I lit an oil lamp and sat down to wait for them.

Blaylocke felt around on the floor, in his pockets, under the bed. He grabbed the overhead crossbeam and pulled himself into a seated position. He narrowed his eyes at me, then glanced around on the floor. "Where is it? I know you took it."

"Get up," I said. "Vilaris and I got into some trouble. Pack your things and gather all the food you can carry. We're abandoning ship."

I packed my own bag, then climbed to the deck to look out for Vilaris. He hadn't returned after another fifteen minutes, by which time Blaylocke and Chaz had joined me above. The crowds below the cliffside elevators were beginning to clear out as night descended, and the winds howling through the canyon put a chill in the air. Many of the fires around us had gone out, leaving the twin cities to gleam on their perches far in the distance.

Seeing my chance, I slipped belowdecks. A rush of warm air assailed me when I entered the furnace room. The potbelly's slatted iron door squealed as I opened it to reveal the warm embers within. I took out the sub-signal remote and split it open with a chisel, ripped out its guts, and tossed the remains onto the fire. *No more crackler. No more listening in while I piss and brush my teeth. They have no choice but to trust me the rest of the way.* I threw another shovelful of coals into the furnace and was back on deck in under a minute.

Vilaris jogged out of the darkness and climbed aboard. "I found a boat. It's not as big as we wanted, and the crew's small too, but it's something. Oh, I should also mention that there are police officers roaming the airfield, looking for us. It took me a long time to get back because I had to dodge them."

"How far away is the ship?" I asked. "I'm just wondering if we should try bringing some of the supplies and food with us."

Vilaris ran a hand through his hair. In the moonlight, I could see a sheen of sweat glistening on his forehead. "We loaded the *Clarity* with enough food to last us three weeks. Chaz has all kinds of tools and tech stuffed away in there, too. I don't see a reason not to bring a little of it, if we can. The ship is further out, fifty yards or so from the aft edge of Mallentis. That way." He pointed.

Blaylocke grabbed my arm. "Get inside. Clint, you too. Cops are coming."

We hurried down the stairs and into the ship. When I glanced back, Blaylocke was standing on deck with his hands at his sides, fists clenched, taking a deep, calming breath. Chaz was hunkered down in the stairwell, staying out of sight. *My fate is now in the hands of a guy who hates my guts*, I realized.

The furnace room was still warm when Vilaris and I entered. The new coals were glowing red above a layer of white powder, and there was a burning plastic smell in the air.

"What *is* that?" Vilaris said, wrinkling his nose.

I changed the subject. "This couldn't get much worse, could it?" I said. "I'm sorry for being a wanted man. This is more trouble than you deserve."

"Gareth won't give us away," Vilaris said. "There are times when his being uptight isn't such a bad thing."

Muffled voices came from above, reverberating along the rafters. A smooth, no-nonsense cop's voice. Blaylocke's cocksure drone. Another cop. Blaylocke again. "You're welcome, officers. I'll be sure to let you know if I see anything."

"This is bad," I said.

"It sounds like they're going away," said Vilaris.

"They want us to think so. No cop gives up that easily. That customs officer by the elevators recognized me on sight. There must be posters of me floating around all over the place. A reward for my capture, maybe. What would be worse is if some officer up there thinks he hit you with one of those pulser rounds and you didn't fall down. Either they'll think you've got some sweet new tech that protects your whole body from pulsers, or they'll figure out you're a primie."

Vilaris's face hardened. "Okay, screw the supplies. Let's just lock up what we can and come back for it later."

"No arguments here."

Chaz was still crouched in the stairwell when I opened the door, clutching the bag he'd packed. Blaylocke was standing on deck, stiff and unmoving, his back to us.

Chaz looked as scared as I'd ever seen him. More scared than the day I met him, right after he'd found out I was a murderer. "Gareth told the officers he was waiting for his shipmates to get back with food. Said he'd keep an eye out for any suspicious characters that came by."

"Why are *you* hiding?" I asked.

"In case we had to run."

"We do," I said. "Those cops aren't gonna give up until they find me."

"I know," Chaz said. "They're still standing right there. They're on the bluewave, talking to headquarters about something."

We listened.

The cop was talking in that smug, cavalier way law-lovers so often do. "... airship, approximately thirty feet, lone passenger says he has shipmates who have not returned. Refuses to allow us to search the vessel. Asking permission to board."

We all heard it. We exchanged looks.

"We have to go now," I said. "The hole in the side of the hull is our only way out from belowdecks."

Vilaris stopped me. "What about Gareth?"

*What about him?* I wanted to say. I thought for a moment. "How many cops are there, Chaz?"

"Two."

"Vilaris... go down and throw a big pile of coals in the furnace. The *Clarity* is taking off... one last time. Meet us in the control capsule."

I can only imagine how surprised Blaylocke must've been a minute or two later when the deck lurched beneath his feet. I was busy below, opening the ballonet valves and cranking the engines to full vertical. I hopped off my chair and grabbed my pack as I felt the ground pull away. When Chaz and Vilaris joined me, we hopped out through the gash and hustled off into the shadows, even as the deck began to ring out with the sounds of the cops' boots.

Taking cover behind a nearby airship, we waited for Blaylocke. I figured he'd build up the gumption to disembark sooner or later. It turned out to be sooner. When we saw him hit the ground, we waved our hands and whispered insults at him until we got his attention.

The last time I ever laid eyes on her, *The Secant's Clarity* was putting on a brave performance, making her cumbersome rise from the floater and giving the cops a bear of a time trying to bring her back down. She drifted backward through the sea of ships at rest, bouncing off hulls and masts until she'd risen high enough to clear them. I wondered how long it was going to take those law-lovers to figure out we were using the ballonets for hot-air lift instead of cold-air ballast. Thinking about it still makes me laugh.

Vilaris led us to the far outskirts of the airfield. We were so close to the aft of the floater that it felt like the stream was going to suck me off the edge if I didn't keep two feet on the ground. The city lights were distant and diffused, lost in a haze of nighttime clouds. I searched the sky for the *Clarity*, but either she'd been swept away into the gloom, or the cops had grounded her somewhere in the airfield.

It was there, on that remote corner of Mallentis, that we first met the *Galeskimmer* and her crew. She was a beauty of a streamboat, slender and flat-bottomed, with a pair of silver turbines and a single sail for riding with the wind. Nothing close to the size or power of my *Ostelle*—she was even shorter than *The Secant's Clarity*—but for our purposes, she'd serve just fine.

We had only the clothes on our back and the belongings in our bags. It was a good thing, too, as we soon found out. The *Galeskimmer* had only one deck and twice as many crewmembers as the *Clarity*. Now that we were coming aboard, she'd have triple the *Clarity*'s crew, in total.

"These are my friends," Vilaris said when we arrived, flushed and out of breath.

"Captain Sable Brunswick, at your service." The voice was strong, bolder somehow than the mouse of a woman who owned it. She was short and thin, all pep and sparkle as she swung down from the deck and gave us a low bow that felt excessive under the circumstances. Her hair was tied back in a simple dirty-blond braid beneath the plumed tricorn she removed when she greeted us. The vest she wore was loose, and the pants that looked as though they had once hugged her slender hips were roomy.

"*Acting*... Captain," said the elderly fellow who emerged after her. He was tall and sinewy, his mouth puckered up tight beneath a snowy white beard, his clothes in need of mending.

Sable gave the old man a look, her blue eyes as sharp as daggers. "Allow me to introduce Landon Scofield, the *Galeskimmer*'s quartermaster and a constant thorn in my side," she told us. "We hear you're in need of a lift."

She was looking at me, so I answered. "If she's fast. Looks like she's got it where it counts."

The Captainess smirked. "Who... me, or the ship?"

"Don't flatter yourself, lady," I said. "There'll be plenty of time for me to tell you how great you are, if you can prove it."

"I've never been one for games, Mr..."

I gave Vilaris a sideways look. "Call me Nordstrom."

Sable wasn't fooled. "Well Mr. Nordstrom, I don't like games, so let's put it all out on the table, shall we? I think you'd better take a look at this."

She shoved a sheet of curled parchment toward me. I took it from her and unrolled it. There I was, WANTED. They'd even included my middle name. I didn't even know I *had* a middle name. Thanks to those law-loving parents of mine, the whole stream knew it now.

"This is a terrible picture," I said. "Who'd the Civs hire to draw this, a blind monkey?"

"An imperfect likeness, maybe," said Sable. "But it's you, nevertheless. Do you see the number at the bottom of the page?"

I nodded. It was a big number.

"Times are hard, Mr. Nordstrom. My crew and I don't have the luxury of doing pro bono work."

"You can pro bono whoever you want," I said. "That's none of my business. All I want to know is how much you charge."

"We fly for whoever's paying the most," said Sable. "Having seen that number there, you now know how much you're worth to the Civil Regency Corps. Would you care to make me an offer?"

"That many chips, plus one," I said.

"There will be additional expenses if we have to fly you halfway across the stream. Then again, tying you up and waiting for the Civvies only costs me a length of rope and a few minutes' time. Try again, Mr. Nordstrom."

"Give me a moment with my colleagues, here," I said. I turned around and we huddled up. "They're your chips, guys. What do you think?"

"Offer her fee-and-a-half," Vilaris said. "The highest I want to go is double."

I spun on my heel. "This much, plus... half this much," I announced, pointing to the number on my wanted poster.

Sable considered this. "How far do you want to go?"

"Get us to the northern fringe. Word doesn't spread so fast out there."

"I wouldn't bet on it, but... throw in another five thousand and you've got yourself a deal," said Sable. "Half upfront, the other half on delivery."

I waited for Vilaris to nod. "We have an agreement." I extended my hand, and Sable slid hers into mine. Her grip was firm, but the bones were like twigs.

"Let me introduce you to the rest of the crew," she said.

The others had gathered on deck to get a look at us. I counted them out. Seven in all, including Sable and Mr. Scofield, the first mate. The other five were just as tattered and thin, but hard and scrappy-looking for all that. There was the paunch-bellied boatswain, Dennel McMurtry, graying beneath his black top-hat, with two gold teeth and tobacco stains over the rest; half-blind rigger Thorley Colburn, a patch-eyed hulk of a man with a hook nose and silver rings through his ears, his clear blue eye shining through a curtain of blond hair; Eliza Kinally, a redhead with wide hips and sharp green eyes, stout and plain; and little Neale Glynton, the dark-haired cabin boy of no more than twelve, bug-eyed and scrawny as a starved cat. The fifth was a skittish little creature called a duender, hardly taller than a child, with a broad hunchback and pointed ears that curved out from the sides of its head like fishing poles. It had a wide, flat nose, and teeth like mallet heads. It was a 'he,' they said, and they called him Nerimund.

The crew helped us aboard and showed us to our bunks. The ship had a surprising amount of room to spare below, and I got the impression that their crew had once been much bigger. They were a ragged lot, and it was clear they needed our money as much or more than we needed their boat. I tossed my things into the hammock little Neale had pointed out to me and climbed above to watch us lift off. I felt no sense of safety, not even packed away on a little ship and bound for a slower part of the stream. I wouldn't feel any more at ease until we'd gone airborne.

I joined Mr. Scofield on the quarterdeck and stood by as Sable took the helm. Thorley Colburn was unfurling the sail while Eliza Kinally and Dennel McMurtry made ready to lash it down. Sable gave the lift controls a tug, and I heard the familiar, repetitive *clink-clink* of the gravstone counterbalances being released. We heaved upward, not smoothly, and Sable blushed as she spun the wheel and turned us leeward. The sail billowed, then snapped tight, and the wind pulled us away from Mallentis.

Mr. Scofield shivered. "Permission to go below, captain."

"Granted," Sable said.

I stayed with her, watching while the dim airfield fires and the bright city lights of Eulaya and Hibantya faded into the clouds. I knew I might never see either of those cities again, but somehow

I didn't mind. We were about to go sailing, and suddenly it was all I could think about.

There are lots of things people seem to think are essential to living a full life. They'll say things like, '*you haven't lived until you've done this*.' Feeling the clouds in your hair on driftmetal runners is one of those things. It's an experience like nothing else. It's like walking on a cloud that's as hard as stone and lighter than the very air you're breathing. Drifting through the darkness on the *Galeskimmer* that evening, I felt as alive as I'd ever been.

"Why did you ask me for my name if you already knew it from the posters?" I asked, turning toward Sable.

"I wanted to know what kind of person you were."

"And what did my answer tell you?"

"That you're a coward and a criminal, just like your wanted poster says."

"Guilty on both counts," I admitted, shrugging.

"You don't seem to mind being an outlaw. Doesn't it ever bother you, knowing you're the scum society has to scrape off its shoe?"

"I haven't always been like this. I used to make an honest living. Then one day, the Regency came along and took my dad's shop. Didn't say why, just shoved a bunch of chips in his face and told him to get lost. We built a boat together, and I aimed to leave home and make my own way in the stream. Problem was, my parents decided they had nothing better to do and came with me."

Sable took a deep breath, the corner of her mouth crinkling. "There are worse problems to have," she said.

"Not for me. My parents are a couple of law-loving... they're traitors. I would've gotten away clean if it weren't for them. They took my boat and handed me over to the Civs. Thinking I could trust them not to get in my way is the stupidest thing I've ever done."

"Taking you aboard is the stupidest thing *I've* ever done. I wouldn't have even entertained the idea if we didn't need the chips so badly."

"You all look like you could use a few chips," I said. I looked around. "So does your rig."

"It's been hard times these last few months."

"Why's that? There's always plenty of hauling to do where I come from, lots of people who need to travel."

"A few months back, we got caught in a big thunderstorm. We lost half our cargo and the storm disabled the *Galeskimmer*. When we showed up late and without the full haul, we ended up losing money on the trip. A lot of money. Uncle Angus was captain before me. He had to go and ask our patrons for some extra time to pay them back. They're not the most savory characters, and instead of giving it to him, they just... took him. Put him in their own debtor's prison of sorts. We've been trying to earn enough to keep the boat working, put food on the table, and save up every extra chip so we can pay off the debt and get Uncle Angus back. It's been hard enough just making ends meet."

There was pain brewing beneath the surface of Sable's eyes. The big white feather was struggling against the wind to stay in place on her hat. I pursed my lips and rubbed the back of my neck, unsure what to say.

"My uncle has always put the crew first, and business second," Sable said. "He took that job because we were all behind him. We knew how dangerous it would be if things went wrong."

"Your uncle is a better man than I," I said.

"You don't much want to be a better man, do you?"

"No, not really," I said.

Sable smirked. "I might be among the minority, but I'm of the opinion that people can change. You've done some bad things, but there's no reason you can't turn yourself around."

"Yeah... I wish the Civs shared your benevolent spirit. I've done a few too many bad things to convince them I deserve anything but a conviction."

"Don't treat yourself like a lost cause," said Sable. "Too many people get stuck letting their mistakes define who they are. However bad your situation might be, you're not powerless. You just have to ask yourself what it's going to take for you to stop playing the role of the delinquent and start having more respect for yourself. To know you can be better."

"I think it's a little too late for that," I said.

Sable disagreed. "It's not up to you, or the Civs, or anyone else, to decide how many misdeeds are too many. Do you think an abundance of small wrongs ever adds up to one big one? Does telling a thousand lies ever become worse than taking someone's life?"

I wasn't much for philosophizing, so I just shrugged.

"Did you ever consider the kind of position you put your parents in, asking them to choose between you and the law? That was your first mistake, the way I see it. You've got to start thinking about how your actions are affecting the people around you."

"I don't gotta do jack," I said. "And I'm not paying you for morality lessons, either."

"You're not paying me at all—your friends are. Friends who obviously see something in you, to stick around."

*They see a meal ticket in me, same as you*, I almost said. But I couldn't go any further without telling her about Pyras and Gilfoyle and the gravstone—much more than I wanted her to know. So I shrugged again and said, "Yeah. I guess."

Mallentis was long gone over the stern, lost in a sea of swirling clouds.

"Well… I'd better get some shuteye. 'Night," I said, clunking down the stairs to the main deck.

"Mulroney," said Sable.

I stopped, trying not to grin. As far as she knew, the full name on the wanted poster was what I went by all the time. "Yeah," I said.

"The minute you step off this boat, you can be whatever kind of person you want to be. While you're aboard, spare me and my crew the ordeal of having to babysit you."

I turned back to her, annoyed but trying not to let it show. "Call me Muller."

Sable's eyes were cold, but not unkind. She gave a slight, almost imperceptible nod.

I trudged below and flung myself into my hammock, exhausted. A chorus of snores and strange smells engulfed me as I lay staring at the ceiling, my bed swaying gently as the ship staggered through the sky. I wondered if every day from now on would be like this one had; filled with the constant stress of running away from a series of narrow escapes. *I'll run from the Civs 'til the day I die*, I promised myself. *The day they catch me is the day Muller Jakes loses*. I fell asleep trying not to think about my life's grim prognosis or the impossible tasks that faced me. Most of all, I tried not to think about what Sable had said.

# 7

I woke with a drumming in my head. I opened my eyes. A finger was tapping the middle of my forehead, slow and rhythmic, like drips from a leaky faucet. I grabbed the hand and pulled it away. Neale Glynton, the cabin boy, was standing there with a stupid grin on his face, bits of food still stuck in his teeth.

"What the hell, kid?"

"You missed breakfast," Neale said. "Time for chores."

"I'm a passenger," I said. "Passengers don't do chores."

Dennel McMurtry, the top-hat-wearing boatswain with all blackened teeth except his two gold ones, was standing behind Neale at the bottom of the stairs. "You paid us enough to keep your identity to ourselves, Mr. Nordstrom," he said in his gruff morning voice. "Sleep costs extra."

I rolled over in my hammock so I was facing the wall, lifted a hand to swat them away. "You heard him, Vilaris. Pay the man."

"Mr. Vilaris and your other friends have been awake since

dawn," said Dennel. "They've been learning their knots and getting a primer on the *Galeskimmer*'s rigging, sails, and steering. They would've swabbed the decks too, but I insisted they leave that job to the last one awake. On your feet, sailor. Start now, and you may finish before lunchtime."

I lifted my hand again, this time using it to make a less polite gesture.

"Is that so, Mr. Nordstrom? If we have a problem, I'm sure I can make an inquiry as to Mr. Scofield's mood this morning. You'll soon find out how he feels about freeloaders."

"I'm sleeping," I said. "Get lost."

I heard them leave.

I was just beginning to drift off to sleep again when a hand collared me and hauled me out of my hammock. I hit the floor with a thud, the planks smacking my elbow and tailbone a good one each. I craned my neck as the big hand and its owner dragged me across the cabin and up the stairs without stopping to give me a chance to stand. Half-blind Thorley Colburn tossed me onto the deck and stepped on my chest when I tried to rise. Everyone was there, to my chagrin; the whole crew, along with Chaz, Blaylocke, and Vilaris.

"This is the one who thinks he's earned himself a free ride."

Old Landon Scofield stood in front of the crowd, thoughtful, the razor-thin filaments of an electroscourge dangling from his wrist port. "I'll give him what he's earned, alright."

I sighed. "Okay, this is all very theatrical of you, but I catch your drift now. Will you stop?"

"Lash him to the mast," said Scofield.

Thorley lugged me to my feet and shoved me toward the center of the boat. Now I was angry. I decided I'd give them one last chance to give up the prank.

"I said... I get it. You can lay off."

Thorley pulled my arms around the mast and began to bind my wrists with a length of thick rope. When I tried to back away, a shoulder pinned me to the mast from behind. I knew it was Dennel McMurtry by the sweet tobacco stench of his breath.

I triggered my wrist spikes and slashed the rope, bringing my elbow back in the same motion to smash Dennel's jaw and drive the spike into his thigh. He hollered and fell over, holding his leg.

I swung myself around the mast like a pole dancer and thrust a foot toward Thorley's face, aiming to blacken his good eye. Instead he caught my ankle between two muscled forearms and dragged me to the ground.

The rest of the crew was on me before I could get to my feet. A weight drove my face into the deck. Someone gathered my legs together and began to bind them. I was under a pile of bodies, kicking and swinging at any flesh I could sink a blow into. *Where are Chaz and Vilaris?* I thought. *Why are they letting this happen?* I figured Blaylocke had been aching to get a few shots in on me, and I wouldn't be surprised if he'd decided to help the crew. People were trying to restrain my limbs. When I struck out with my climbing spikes, they grabbed my arms and pinned them to the deck. Soon I heard voices over the din.

"Let him up. Let him up," Vilaris was shouting.

"Get off him," Chaz said, shoving the cabin boy off my back.

I rolled over and pushed myself up, backed away so there was no one behind me. "I'm not part of your blasted crew," I said, wiping away the sting of sweat and wood splinters. "Fly your own ship. Swab your own bloody deck."

It wasn't until I'd gotten a good look around that I realized it wasn't me everyone was staring at. It was Blaylocke. Sometime during the melee, the sleeve of his jacket had been ripped open.

I still didn't know whether he'd been on the crew's side or mine, but blood was dripping from a wound in his arm. Primie blood, the deep scarlet color of a ripe red apple. Dennel McMurtry's pants were stained a dark blue-violet from the wound I'd given him—the color of a techsoul's blood.

The crew was aghast—Sable most of all. She was scalding me with those thin hazel eyes, skeptical. "Is this why the Regency is after you? You're primitives? No, that can't be... you have augments." She touched a finger to her wrist, recalling my spikes. There was a broad knifeblade jutting out from her wrist, an augment of her own. "Which of you are primitives? Just you?"

Vilaris spoke up. "If it's money you want, we can pay you more chips to—"

"This goes beyond what chips can cover," Sable said. "This is treachery of the highest order."

"The highest," Nerimund chimed in, peeking out from behind Sable's arm.

"Primitives are people, living their lives, just like you are," I said. "So what if they bleed a different color? So what if they're not synthetic? Does that make us any better?" I hesitated. "Alright... so technically, we're better, speaking from a purely physical perspective. I'll concede that point. But we're still the same species."

I didn't know why I was standing up for them. It's not like I cared about primies all that much. Maybe I'd started to like Chaz and Vilaris somewhere along the line without realizing it. I'm many things, but a genocidal maniac isn't one of them.

"Do you have any idea how much more danger we've unwittingly put ourselves into by harboring primitives?" said Sable. "Aiding a wanted felon is one thing. Filling the ship with primitives is another gamble entirely. There are people who would slaughter us all if they found out we were primie sympathizers."

"Yeah, we do know the risks," I said. "That's why we were trying to keep it a secret."

Sable let out a sigh. "You know the Regency's stance against primitives. I cannot, in good conscience, submit my crew to a situation as unsafe as this."

"Then stop listening to your conscience," I said. "And listen to your gut."

Sable gave me a mocking smile. "They're the same thing."

"Wrong. Your conscience tells you what you're *supposed* to do. Your gut tells you what you know is right."

"I always do the right thing," she said. "And the right thing is keeping my crew and my ship intact, whatever it takes. As much as I want to get Uncle Angus back, the *Galeskimmer* is our home. I won't allow you to stay in our home if it's against the crew's wishes. We'll let them decide." Sable's wrist blade *shwicked* away into her arm. "All in favor of keeping our passengers onboard, raise your hand."

No one did.

Sable waited a long moment, looking over each of her companions to be sure. "All opposed?"

Every hand shot up, including Sable's.

Vilaris sighed and ran a hand through his greasy hair. Chaz hung his big white bandaged head. Blaylocke was clutching his arm, his jaw set tight. I imagined their stomachs were sinking, like mine was.

"You have your answer, Muller Jakes. We'll let you off at the next stop. I'll refund the unused portion of your deposit then, minus expenses."

"Who has your Uncle?" I said.

Sable narrowed her eyes at me. "Maclin Automation," she said.

*Interesting*, I thought. *This has some legs. Literally.* "The augmentation research and development company?"

"You're familiar with them, I'm sure."

"Are you kidding? Half the tech in my body is Maclin stuff. Well, not anymore." I gave Chaz an apologetic look. "But I used to have lots of Maclin-made augments. They kidnapped your uncle? Really? What's a big conglomerate like that doing maintaining its own off-the-record debtor's prison?"

"I don't know the extent of Uncle Angus's business relationship with Maclin. But they told me if I reported them to the Regency, it was the last time I'd ever see him. There's nothing we can do about it except pay them what they ask."

"Whatever you dropped from that shipment must've been pretty important to get them so upset with you. Too bad it's lost to the Churn by now, or sitting smashed up on some floater. How much do they want, if you don't mind me asking?"

"They said the part of the shipment we lost was worth three hundred thousand chips. They want three-fifty, including interest and damages that resulted from the loss."

"Dear sweet merciful Leridote." I scratched my noggin, trying to stimulate the idea that was growing in my brain-cavity. "Have you paid them anything yet?"

"Nothing. We still haven't repaired all the damage to the *Galeskimmer*. The other half of your fee would've gotten us over the top and started us well on our way in the savings department."

I looked at my companions. Chaz was still looking a little spacey, still coming back from that nasty knock to the head. Blaylocke was leaning against the ship's railing with his arms folded in front of him, holding a strip of cloth to his wound.

Vilaris was giving me that squirrely look of his, the one that says, *'don't do what I think you're about to do, or I'll lose it.'*

I flashed Vilaris a sly grin and cleared my throat. "I can't help but feel like this partnership has started off on the wrong foot. Let's let bygones be bygones and start over, shall we? We're going to be working together very closely over the next few weeks, and I want everyone here getting along. We need to be a well-oiled machine if we're going to do this—"

Sable's knifeblade flicked out again. She took two quick strides toward me and jerked the blade up to my throat. "What in the *heavens'* name are you going on about?" she said.

I winked at her. "We're partners now, you and I. Your crew and mine."

"I'm afraid you are very much mistaken," she said.

"Am I? I don't think so. You see, by the time you manage to scrape together three hundred and fifty thousand chips, your Uncle Angus will be a skeleton. Shoot, *I'll* be an old man by then. Call me a fool for overlooking it until now, but it's just become startlingly apparent to me how much we need each other."

"We don't need the likes of you, or your primitives, to blacken our good name."

"Well then, let me tell you what *I* need," I said. "I need a ship. This one will do the trick. I need my friends to be protected by a good group of upstanding techsouls. Case in point." I waved a hand toward her crew. "And last, I need to find a certain gentleman by the name of Alastair Gilfoyle. When you help us find him and take back what's ours, this life of indentured servitude you're leading will be over. Because in exchange for helping us, I'm going to offer you half my share of the takings."

Vilaris scrunched up his face. "*Your* share? Since when do *you* have a share?"

"Since I agreed to launch this little excursion for you, Clint. You told me I would be paid for my troubles. As payment, I want a one-quarter share of the haul, to split with the fine folks who live and work on the *Galeskimmer*."

"You can't take *that much* of the city's income," Vilaris blurted out.

"I can, and I will. It's a one-fourth share or it's nothing at all."

"Wait a minute... what city?" said Mr. Scofield.

I grasped for words. "The city we're all from. Bannock," I lied.

"Bannock is no city. It's a drift-town, at best."

"We call it a city sometimes. Give us a break." I turned to Sable, desperate to change the subject. "Captain Brunswick... do you and your crew *really* want to spend the next several years of your lives scraping by, trying to earn enough to pay your debts? Or would you rather help us and get your uncle back right away? Don't delude yourself. This is going to take a lot longer than you're willing to admit, unless you help us."

Sable lowered her blade. She took off her hat, wiped the sweat from her brow with a thin white shirtsleeve. When she spoke, she was addressing her crew. "You all heard him. We have a long road ahead of us if we go it alone. Getting Captain Angus back means making sacrifices. Knowing what we know now changes things. All in favor of combining crews and working together for a short period of time, raise your hand." She counted. "All opposed?" She counted again, then looked at me. "The matter appears to be settled, Mr. Nordstrom."

This time, old Landon Scofield and young Eliza Kinally were the only ones who had voted against us. I hadn't heard a word out of Eliza's mouth since we'd been on board. I didn't even know what job she had on the ship. But it was apparent that, for any number of available reasons, she didn't like us.

"Good," I said. "This is surely the start of a very lucrative and prosperous arrangement. We need to fire up the turbines and set a course upstream if we're going to find Gilfoyle."

The crew glared at me.

"Not an order," I said, "just a suggestion. Now if you'll excuse me, I'll be getting back to bed."

I caught another handful of dirty looks as I made my way belowdecks. *They can hate me if they want to,* I told myself as I crawled into my hammock. *They can keep on hating me after I make them filthy rich, for all I care. Just as long as they don't treat me like some lowborn swabbie. I've been captain of my own boat, for crying out loud. One day, I'll retake command of my* Ostelle. *Nobody will ever order me around again after that.* I drifted off to sleep, my head swelling with pride, eager to dream of all the good things to come.

"I'm impressed." My eyes shot open at the sound of Sable's voice. I found her standing beside my hammock, a hand on her hip. "Not many people can twist a hopeless situation to their advantage like you can."

I yawned and stretched. "Yeah, well, I'm not many people. And you're no fool, either. You caught on to how impressive I am without a single hint. Usually I have to spell it out for people."

Sable's hand was at my throat. No blade this time—just her cold, skinny fingers. She was doing a fair job of convincing me that she was not a friendly person.

"I thought I told you to behave yourself while you were aboard my ship," she said.

I tried to gulp, but the lump didn't make it past her grip. "I was behaving myself just fine. Then they dragged me out of bed for a whipping I didn't deserve. That isn't a situation I'm comfortable *behaving* for."

"Why didn't you just follow orders?"

"Following orders would suggest that I'm a lesser being than the person who's giving them," I said. "I'm no slave, sister. I'm your cargo, not your hired hand."

"Oh, you're our cargo, are you? Maybe we ought to find a nice big empty crate to shove you into."

"If it's the only way I can get a decent night's sleep without you jerkwads being all over my case about it..."

She tightened her grip on my throat and leaned in. Her braid slipped around her back and fell onto my lap with a *whop*. I could smell her, the faint animal scent of unwashed woman beneath layers of perfume.

"I don't care how much you're worth to us," she said. "This can be an easy trip for you. Keep on provoking me, and I'll see that it's a hard one. Up to you."

I kissed her. Wrapped my hand around the back of her head and pulled her in tight. She shrieked into my open mouth, wrenched away, punched me high on the cheekbone. The blow left me stinging, and a little stunned as well. Probably no more stunned than I'd made her.

"You asshole," she shouted. She was seething, nostrils flared, face flushed as purple as a beet.

On a good day, that kiss would've been a love story in the making. Today, it was just a guy distracting a girl from choking him to death. I'll admit it wasn't the most elegant way of achieving the desired effect. But when you wake up to find an angry woman threatening to cause you harm, you only have so many options.

"Ow," I said, rubbing my cheek. "I'm sorry... I don't know what came over me. I just... couldn't control myself a minute longer." I might've pulled off the sentiment, if I hadn't been laughing.

"If you *ever* lay a finger on me again, I'll have Mr. Scofield beat you so good you'll forget how to bleed." There wasn't an ounce of joviality in her. I didn't realize she'd triggered the blade until I heard it slide back in, just before she stormed out of the cabin.

I couldn't sleep after that. I couldn't go above and face her either, so I stayed in my hammock, staring at the ceiling and wondering if there was a way to make this boat go any faster. I wanted to be done with this. Done with them, and *her*. Sable had made it clear that she wanted nothing to do with me. The sooner my companions and I could get out of her hair, the better.

The *Galeskimmer* turned into the wind that day. Instead of moving toward the fringe to escape the Regency's influence, we were heading straight into the heart of the stream, where drifting cities and massive ships crested the clouds at altitudes of tens of thousands of feet.

Vilaris and Blaylocke had their theories about where Gilfoyle might've set up shop, and I had a few of my own. Once we got close, all we'd have to do was ask the locals. Gilfoyle would turn up. You don't relocate a Churn mining operation without getting noticed. Gilfoyle would be hiring workers to replace the ones he'd lost by moving. He'd also be selling his product to people in the stream as their drift-towns passed by. It could take months or years for the lowest floaters to circle Esperon, so townies were often eager to buy from grav platforms when they had the chance.

The tension on board was palpable for the remainder of our journey. Chaz was getting better every day, remembering who he was and becoming more like his old self again. Blaylocke was still a jerk, but the crew's mistrust forced us to put our differences aside and band together. I even bit the bullet and swabbed a few decks. After a day or two, I decided I didn't want to feel bad about kissing Sable anymore, so I got over it. She didn't, though.

*J.C. Staudt*

We stopped twice during the trip for fuel and supplies. The first time was on a thickly wooded floater with gargantuan saibon trees called Lorehawke; the second was on Jaddow's Bluff, an oddly-shaped drift-town that looked like a jagged ice cream cone with half the scoop missing.

On our ninth day out from Mallentis, Mr. Scofield guided the *Galeskimmer* through a fluffy carpet of clouds and brought us into a calm breeze near the Knuckles—half a dozen drift-towns joined together by a series of bridges. From above, they looked almost like the strands of a spiderweb, a loose network of nodes and synapses.

The Knuckles had been the invention of one Richard Wainsborough; his means of solving the problem of owning several floaters that required air travel to go between. Through great expenditure and hassle, he'd had them pushed together and joined by lengths of thick, flexible metal cable. Crossing one of the bridges when the winds were high was hardly safer than walking a tightrope, so most people simply didn't. Wainsborough was long dead, and his islands had passed into the hands of his descendants, who'd parceled out various plots and sold them to private owners. The current residents considered living so close to other drift-towns little more than a fortunate convenience. As yet, no one had bothered to go to the trouble or expense of removing the bridges, and so there the islands remained, tied to one another.

We landed on an island called Falkombe, one of the larger floaters in the chain. It was egg-shaped and hilly, with wide expanses of field, tall grasses and gnarled riverwood trees. When the wind was just right, you'd get the swampy stench of its nearest neighbor, Dunhollow, a larger island with little in the way of habitable area. Dunhollow had inward-sloping terrain and soft soil, so it held rainwater like a sponge and was covered in marshes and bayous. Wainsborough had fancied himself quite the seafarer, and he'd had a large set of docks and boathouses built on Dunhollow. By now, most of those structures had fallen into disrepair.

It was on Falkombe that we found our first sign of Gilfoyle: four deep, round imprints in a gravel parking lot outside the general store. I recognized the imprints as being the exact same size and configuration as the hovertrucks the miners used. The gouges were severe, and I surmised that the vehicle which had made them was not only heavy and cumbersome; it had been carrying a full load. I scooped up a handful of gravel and sniffed it. *Displacer engines... no doubt about that.*

"You were right, Blaylocke," I said. "As much as I hate to admit it, you were right. Gilfoyle is close."

Blaylocke tried to make his smile look like a grimace. He squinted up at the clouds, a leaden matte that blotted out the sun. The day was cool and windy, the skies threatening rain, and the air dense with the fetid smell of Dunhollow's swamps. Captain Sable had sent Thorley Colburn, the broad-shouldered rigger, along with us—to '*help out*,' as she put it. She'd really sent him to keep an eye on us, of course, and had kept Vilaris on board to talk over a few financial matters related to our agreement. I would've stayed to attend the meeting, but I got the feeling Sable would've ignored me or excluded me from it entirely if I had. Besides, I was too hot on Gilfoyle's trail at the moment to be bothered with the finer points of our contract. I'd seen these hovertruck imprints from the deck before we landed, and I'd been dying to get out here for a closer look.

Chaz was wearing his mad-scientist goggles, complete with a selection of concentric glass lenses for light filtering and magnification. He flicked one aside, lowered another into place. "These are incredible specimens," he was saying, as his gigantic eyeball darted over a palmful of gravel. The bulging oculus was red-veined and wet with rheum, altogether startling and absurd-looking.

"Chaz, ol' buddy... you get more excited about dirt than most men get about beautiful women," I said.

"There are tiny flecks of driftmetal in a few of these stones," Chaz explained, ignoring me.

Blaylocke was confused. "If there's driftmetal in them, why do they fall to the ground like normal rocks? Why don't they float?"

"Surely your understanding of the properties of driftmetal is better than you're letting on," I said.

"Not really. Why... should it be?"

"Things are different in Py—" Chaz caught himself and glanced across the lot at Thorley, who was kicking divots into the gravel to amuse himself. "—back home, in Bannock."

Blaylocke grinned. "Bannock, yeah."

"It's a matter of mass versus altitude," said Chaz. "In Bannock, we're not used to this because we're so low to the ground. Small chunks of driftmetal like these have a very low point of equilibrium. It sounds counterintuitive, but that's why all the tiny floaters are in the nearflow, while the islands with the largest driftmetal veins are so high up in the stream."

"That's also why all the driftmetal smiths live way up there," I said. "You can't work a big piece of driftmetal while it's floating away from you."

"And yet, isn't it interesting the way driftmetal is affected by gravstone proximity," Chaz observed. "If you think of driftmetal as being like a helium balloon, gravstone is like the ribbon that keeps it from floating away. Streamboats wouldn't exist without the gravstone control arrays that allow them to gain and lose altitude at will."

Blaylocke shrugged. "Whatever you say, Chester. I'm not sure I understand how it all works. As long as you know what you're talking about, I'm satisfied."

"Yeah, speaking of that," I said, "what's a technotherapist?"

"What makes you bring that up?" Chaz asked.

"You're a tinker. A gadgeteer. And the sign outside your lab at home says you're the city's Chief Technotherapist."

"It means I acclimate citizens to the ideas behind new technology. That's all."

"Kind of like what you're unsuccessfully doing for Blaylocke right now," I said.

Chaz laughed. "Indeed."

"Alright, I'm going inside," I said. "Do you guys mind staying with Kicks McGee over there and keeping him out of trouble?"

They said they didn't, so I knelt and rubbed dirty smudges into my face and my clothes. I swung the door open and entered the general store, a drab old establishment called Windmast & Co. The proprietor was a plump little man with a dark handlebar moustache and round pink cheeks that held up a thin pair of spectacles. He was dressed in a pristine vest suit and a matching black bowler hat that covered his bald spot. His well-groomed appearance belied the stuffy odor of his store, which smelled like it hadn't had a good cleaning in years.

"How d'you do?" I said, nodding to him. I pretended to peruse some of the dusty old crap I had no interest in, not wanting to appear too eager to interrogate the guy.

"May I help you with anything, sir?"

"Just looking," I said. After a minute or two, I approached the counter.

He looked up from the newspaper he was reading and studied me through the top half of his bifocals. Something in his stare made me think I was familiar to him, like he'd seen me before. On a wanted poster, probably.

"'Scuse me," I said. "I come here looking for a job."

"I'm sorry sir, but we aren't hiring."

"Oh, my apologies. Not to work *here*. Y'see, I'm a miner by trade. Worked the nearflow all my life. Trawlers, diggers, catchers, grinders—you name it, I can run it. Heard there was a new game in town... someone settin' up nearby." I put a little extra drawl into it, selling the hillbilly laborer persona.

The proprietor gave me a look of understanding. "Yes, you are quite correct. There's an operation, name of Gilfoyle and Associates, something or other. They've been around here a week or so. We're just downstream of them now. If you have a way to get down, head southwest and you should see the platforms not more than a few miles out."

"Well I sure am grateful to you," I said. "Say, I noticed you was sold out of them fancy neckties back there. The brown ones."

"I'm sorry? Oh, the cravats, you mean..."

"Them's the ones. You think I'd put on a good impression if I was wearin' one of them for my interview? It'd be real nice if I could look sharp when I go in. I don't s'pose it'd be too much of a bother if I asked you to take a look in your stock room, in case there's any extra you might've missed."

The man blinked, giving me a tight-lipped smile. "I don't believe those are in stock, sir, but I'll certainly take a look. Just a moment, please." He laid his newspaper on the counter, dislodged himself from his stool, and waddled through the doors to the back room.

When I heard him start to shuffle boxes around, I left. On my way out, I tore the wanted poster off the bulletin board beside the door, crumpled it into a ball, and tossed it into the barrel trash can on the porch. "Time to go," I said. "We've got some gravstone to steal."

# 8

Chaz stood and shoved a pebble into his pocket, one bloated eye pulsating behind a triad of lenses. "What did the shopkeep say?"

"We're practically right on top of them. Gilfoyle's new mining operation is less than half an hour away. Dangit, Blaylocke, your nose for finding people appears to be more exceptional than I'm ready to give you credit for. I'm calling it now: this was a fluke."

Blaylocke said nothing as we made our way back to the *Galeskimmer*, but he wasn't fooling anyone with that proud grin he was barely holding back the whole way there. We skirted the town to avoid any other prying eyes who might've seen my wanted poster. By now, I'd be surprised if there was a soul left in the stream who didn't know my middle name, or who hadn't at least seen my unflattering likeness plastered across every town square.

When we boarded the *Galeskimmer*, I headed straight for the captain's quarters and knocked on the door.

"Come in." Sable was lounging in her chair with a glass of wine, the overcast sky filling the room with gloomy gray light. She rolled her eyes and crossed her legs when she saw me, bouncing her foot beneath the table. "What do you want?"

"We're close," I said, letting the door swing shut behind me. "I found out where Gilfoyle is."

She shrugged. "Good for you."

"Are you really still that mad at me?"

She tossed her braid, reached back and checked it with her fingers, chewed on her lip.

I cleared my throat. I'd told myself I wouldn't blunder through this, but dispelling the silence seemed more daunting now than it had been in my imagination. "I'm sorry I... I touched you. Without your permission. I'm sorry I kissed you." I felt my face go hot. "It was inappropriate." I ground my teeth, my chest thumping like a scared rabbit.

The ten-or-so feet of space between us might as well have been a chasm. I didn't know whether I was apologizing because I cared about her, or because I needed something from her. If I were honest with myself, it was probably a little bit of both.

Sable set her glass on the mantle beneath the windows. I expected her to get up, to come toward me. To look at me, at least. She didn't. Just sat there, staring down at her fingernails as though she were as interested in the dirt beneath them as Chaz would've been to find a loose bit of driftmetal there. She still wasn't saying anything.

"And I'm sorry I didn't tell you my friends were primies," I added, hoping it was what she'd been waiting for me to say. Apparently, it wasn't.

"Did you mean it?" she asked.

"Do I mean what?"

"When you kissed me. Did you do it because you wanted to, or because you thought it would get you out of trouble?"

Behind her, the riverwood trees were swaying in the wind, their twisted, sinewy branches heavy with leaves as thick as shrubbery. A light rain began to patter on the windows. I wished I hadn't come—that I had sent Vilaris to deliver the news in my stead so I could be below in my hammock, napping with the crew. It was too hostile for comfort in here. I wanted to lie, to say I'd done it because of the way I felt about her, but I couldn't bring myself to preserve such an empty falsehood. I usually found it much easier to lie to the people who didn't matter. Maybe my hesitance to lie to Sable meant that she was one of the people who did.

"I just wanted to get you off my case," I said.

She nodded. Her lips tightened, a sharp line creasing her brow, and she turned away to stare out the window. She swiveled in her chair until I couldn't see her face anymore. She was quiet for a moment. "We'll wait out the storm and then head down there."

I hesitated. My foot slid half a step toward her, but I didn't let it go any closer.

I tried to be silent as I shut the door behind me and crossed the deck. The rain had become a steady downpour, and I was drenched by the time I reached the stairs and descended to the crew's quarters. They were all inside, my people and the *Galeskimmer*'s, settling in and relishing the opportunity to get some extra leisure time. Neale Glynton was lying on his back, tossing a ball up to ricochet off the bunk above him. Big Thorley Colburn was carving a wooden figure with his rigging knife while Dennel McMurtry read to himself from a thick leatherbound tome with no title on the outside. Nerimund was sitting cross-legged on his bunk, biting his fingernails. Eliza Kinally was banging pots and dishes around in the kitchen, and Mr. Scofield was probably off somewhere studying his navigation charts and updating his maps. Blaylocke was writing letters to his wife, and Chaz was examining the rocks he'd picked up, scribbling notes about them in his journal.

Vilaris was sound asleep. I settled into my hammock and set about joining him.

It rained all afternoon and into the evening. By the time we ventured into the galley for supper, it was past dark. A fog had settled over the fields of Falkombe, shrouding the *Galeskimmer* in its dense blanket. Eliza had made us a hearty stew of carrots, onions and potatoes with chunks of meat, just the thing to warm our bones on a night like this. We'd eaten well since we came aboard; now that the money was flowing, Sable and her crew had bought enough food to keep the ship's larder well-stocked.

After the meal, we paraded across the ship single-file and gathered in the captain's quarters to discuss our plans. Everyone was included—not just those of us making the decisions. I had a role in mind for each person to play. After all, I'd learned the hard way not to get into something this big on my own.

"We have a bead on Gilfoyle's location," I announced. "I say we strike while the iron is hot. Get this done fast, so we can rescue your captain."

"Don't we have to turn the ore into chips first?" asked Landon Scofield.

"Ore into chips. Chips first," said Nerimund.

"Mr. Scofield, that's a very good question. I'll get to that."

He eyed me. "Very well. Then the next order of business is how, exactly, we're to go about this whole ordeal."

"If you'll permit me to share a few of my ideas," I said.

Mr. Scofield nodded. So did Nerimund.

When I glanced in Sable's direction, she was staring at me, as if in a trance. She looked away, snapping out of it.

"You're a talented crew," I told them. "I've seen how well you run this ship. So I want you to do what you do best: fly the *Galeskimmer*, and fly her like there isn't a more noble pursuit in all the world. Mr. McMurtry, how many guns can she bring to bear, and what kind?"

The quartermaster removed his black top-hat and scratched his head. "The guns've been packed away for quite some time now. We don't like to present a threat most times, since we haven't much to support one. I think of the ones we haven't sold, there's an old cannon or two down there. Four-pounders, I believe, plus a barrel of powder and a dozen rounds."

"So no fleckers, lasers... nothing like that," I said, ready to be disappointed.

Dennel shook his head.

"Okay. How many of you are trained to use them?"

"Just me and Cap' Sable," said Dennel. "Thorley here knows how, but... his depth perception ain't the best, you know."

I smiled. "Captain Sable?"

Her eyes were cold blue spheres, but she spoke with courtesy. "I'll help man the guns, if it comes to that."

"In the meantime, they'd better be brought above and set up. I don't think we'll need them, but it couldn't hurt. Eliza, did you pick up everything you needed in town today?"

"Aye," she said, her green eyes smiling.

"Good, good. There's a warehouse on Platform 14 where they keep all the unprocessed ore. It's where I found the gravstone last time. My mistake was not realizing that every hovertruck in the place is bugged. The mine operators want to know which vehicles are being used where, and by stealing the hovertruck itself I unwittingly led them right to me.

"From the warehouse, the ore is taken to Platform 22 to be processed. The layout of the processing plant is pretty complicated, but there's only one section they use to extract gravstone. Whatever gravstone Gilfoyle possesses has to be in one of those two places—Platform 14, or Platform 22—I just don't know which. That means that if my primary plan doesn't work out, we're going to have to strike both at the same time."

A murmur arose among the crew, uneasy words.

"You're wondering how we're gonna pull that off with eleven people and a ship to fly. Easier done than said, I assure you. Alastair Gilfoyle owes the city of Bannock a great deal of money." I made sure I said '*Bannock*' instead of '*Pyras*' this time. "He broke his contract and failed to pay us for services rendered. So before we bother with any of this gravstone heist nonsense, we're going to do what grown men are supposed to do when there's a disagreement. Talk to him, face-to-face."

"Didn't he try to kill you last time?" asked Mr. Scofield.

"Gilfoyle gave the order and his thugs carried it out," I said, nodding. "But if we can get to him when he's not surrounded by his goons, I don't think he'll be in a position to carry out violence."

"Alright, enough," said Sable. "This talk of killing is making me anxious. I hope Gilfoyle agrees to uphold his half of the contract and pay what he owes. There doesn't need to be any more killing going on."

*You're in the wrong profession if you're afraid of killing*, I almost said. "I hope he does, too. But in case he doesn't, here's my idea for a backup plan."

It took two hours for me to explain my idea to the crew and discuss every minor point they were concerned about. We made alterations where necessary, shifting our little skeleton crew around to accommodate the various tasks, and working out a few timing and logistical issues I'd overlooked. I was convinced we were ready, but we'd plotted late into the night and everyone was tired, so we decided to get some rest and execute the scheme the following day.

I didn't sleep much that night, and I got the feeling no one else did either. The rain had stopped by the time we woke, but the sky was gray that morning, and the fog still lay thick in the fields around the *Galeskimmer*. I tried not to think about whether all of us would live to see the end of that day. I didn't want it to matter.

"How you feelin', Chaz?" I asked him over breakfast.

"Ready," he said, biting off half a strip of bacon.

"I'm gonna be counting on you today. Hard."

"I've got everything you asked for. It's all set to go." Chaz's straight black hair had grown out since we'd left Pyras. Now that his head wound had healed and he no longer wore the bandages, he'd taken to sweeping the drape out of his eyes and tying it behind his head, the way Vilaris often did. Chaz would've looked a right sailor if it weren't for those goggles and the gadgets he was always tinkering around with.

I cuffed him on the shoulder and stood to leave. "You're a better man and a better primie than I ever expected to meet," I told him, and meant it.

While I was helping Dennel McMurtry carry one of the four-pounders up the stairs to the deck, Blaylocke passed us, going down. I was pleasantly surprised when he grabbed the middle of the cannon and helped us lug it the rest of the way. The thing was deceptively heavy for its size.

"Thanks," I said, dusting off my hands. "So... have you decided yet?"

He nodded. "I'm coming to Gilfoyle's."

Blaylocke had been unsure whether his skills would be better served on board the *Galeskimmer* in the event that we needed to raid the platforms, or if he should do the brave thing and come with us to confront Gilfoyle. Rather than fighting him over it, I'd left it up to him. Giving Blaylocke a hard time had lost some of its luster. I'd seen the man get more homesick and despondent with each passing day. Instead of the retorts and angry challenges he used to give me, he'd started to ignore me or walk away whenever I tried to start a verbal sparring match with him. It made me feel like a real prick. But I *am* a real prick, so I figure it kept me grounded.

"*Ding-ding-ding,*" I sang. "Correct answer."

"How sure are you that Gilfoyle's going to fold? You think he'll just hand over the chips he owes us?"

"Absolutely not. I think he's gonna be the same old cigar-smoking, medallion-wearing, walking-cane-up-his-butt, ore-smelting donkey. He'll be just as hard to deal with as ever. The only difference is that he won't have his muscle around to give orders to."

"Why are we even trying then? Let's just go straight to Plan B."

I threw up my hands and let them slap my thighs. "There's only so much of this defeatist attitude of yours I can take, Blaylocke. We're trying it this way because... *why not*? And also because, what good are death and destruction if you're not having fun?"

Blaylocke frowned and started to walk away.

"Hey," I said, halting him. "Nobody on this boat is dumb enough not to notice you feeling sorry for yourself all the time.

Except maybe Nerimund. I actually don't know if that guy's dumb or if he just likes repeating what everyone says. Anyway, you're crushing the mood around here. We're supposed to be getting riled up for tonight. The people who crew this ship are a bunch of glorified mailmen; this is the most dangerous thing most of them have probably ever done. But you? You're a City Watchman. You ride hoverbikes across the Churn like it's an ice skating rink, for crying out loud. Take some pride in yourself. You miss your family? Great. When you get home, tell them the stories about how you fought to do right by them, for the good of Pyras—not stories about how you moped around the ship and cried the whole time. We're doing this for them. Well... you are, at least. I'm in it for the chips."

There was the hint of a twinkle in Blaylocke's eye, as if a fond memory had swept over him. He started to walk away again. When he was halfway across the deck, he called back over his shoulder. "Let's not screw this up, blueblood."

I could hear the smile on his face when he said it.

I stood for a moment and looked out across the fields, laden with their thick blanket of fog. Rays of daylight had begun to pierce through. I hoped the sun would burn away the rest and give us clear skies before nightfall.

"Mr. Jakes, if you'll accompany me for a moment..."

I hadn't noticed Landon Scofield approaching, but he was there, standing behind me with a blank look on his face. Nerimund stood behind him, peering out around his arm like a child.

"What is it?"

"Ms. Brunswick would like a word with you."

"A word," said Nerimund.

If I'd had to guess the word Sable wanted to say to me, it wouldn't have been one I enjoyed hearing. Still, I followed Scofield obediently, keeping my distance from the little duender trailing at his heels. Inside the captain's quarters, Sable was standing near her table full of maps and charts. Dennel McMurtry was there too. He was sitting in one of the wooden armchairs, legs pressed together beneath the table, picking at the brim of the top-hat in his lap. His eyes had a cold, glazed look, and worry lines crinkled his forehead.

Sable waited for the door to close. "So, Mr. Jakes. Tell us about Pyras."

I feigned innocence. "What's Pyras?"

"Mr. McMurtry overheard you talking with Mr. Blaylocke outside. You said you were doing this *'for the good of Pyras.'* What does that mean?"

"Just an expression," I said. "It's the name of the company we want to start someday. Once we have the money."

Sable tapped the map on the table with her finger. "Show me where it is."

I lifted an eyebrow. "Where our company is?"

"Where Bannock is. Show me where your home town is on this map."

I crossed the room and stood next to the table, looking down. The winds of the stream were fickle and ever-changing, so the positions and movements of inhabited floaters could only be tracked if they were emitting a bluewave signal. Maps had to be redrawn on a constant basis using the distances estimated by the ship's receivers. The map showed everything on our side of the world, represented by a series of dots, with lines that showed the various distances between them and their average speeds in the stream. There were no altitude markers on most of them, and only a few had names—the ones Mr. Scofield knew from memory or had seen when we'd passed them.

I studied the map for a moment, trying to decide which floater to point to. Everything in the stream had moved since the last time I'd looked at a stream chart, floaters shifting and passing one another in their never-ending cycle around Esperon. In truth, I'd only been to Bannock that one time. So with my limited, out-of-date aerographical knowledge, there were a dozen different points on the map I thought could be Bannock. If we'd really lived there, as I'd told them, it would've been easier to narrow it down.

"That one," I said, pointing.

Sable's eyes followed my hand to the table. Her face hardened. "You're not from Bannock. None of you are."

I might have held up the lie a little longer, but there was no sense in it. The jig was up, and I knew it. "Here's the thing... I may have lied a little." I sucked in a breath, bracing myself.

Sable grimaced, deflated. She was too fed up with me to be enraged. "First it was your name, then the primitives... and now this. Where do the lies stop, Mulroney? Did Gilfoyle *really* steal something from your city—wherever that is—or did he steal it from *you*? Did he even steal anything in the first place? Or was this some elaborate ploy to get us to help you burglarize an innocent man?"

"This is real," I said. "It's the truth. Everything about Gilfoyle is exactly like we've told you it is. He had a contract with Pyras. We don't know whether he broke the contract because crime drove him away, or because he's plotting Pyras's downfall with one of the city's leaders. All we know is that Gilfoyle took their gravstone without paying for it, and now he owes them a lot of money."

Sable's blue eyes searched mine, looking for a shred of truth. "Before we go any further with this, I think it's time you told us about Pyras."

"I can't do that," I said. I was thinking about the day I'd threatened to tell everyone in the stream that Pyras existed. Why did I care so much about Pyras's secrecy now? I should've been looking out for myself, taking every opportunity I had to keep myself out of prison.

"I suggest you do, or the deal is off," said Sable.

"I suggest you do. Deal is off, deal is off," said Nerimund.

"It's not my place," I said. "My friends trusted me to keep it a secret, and I won't betray them. This may be my fault for opening my big mouth, but I don't have the right to explain Pyras on their behalf. They should be the ones to do that."

Sable was still scrutinizing my every word and facial expression. "Those primitives are that important to you," she said, asking.

I didn't know the answer to her question. I knew what she wanted to hear, and I knew I didn't want to piss off anyone else until we were finished with Gilfoyle. "They've kept my secret. Why shouldn't I keep theirs?"

Sable nodded and sent Dennel McMurtry to summon the primies. The three men knew something was wrong as soon as they entered the room, just like I had. Sable was quiet, giving me the opportunity to speak first.

"Fellas," I said, "I'm sorry. Mr. McMurtry overheard Blaylocke and me talking a few minutes ago. They know we're not from Bannock, and they want to know about Pyras. I haven't told them anything because I wanted it to be your choice whether they know or not. The Captain says the deal's off unless somebody comes clean."

Blaylocke looked at me, betrayed. Chaz looked to Vilaris for direction. Vilaris just scratched his dark beard, then tugged at the knot in his tieback to let his hair fall down around his face.

"Pyras is our home—not Muller's," said Vilaris. "We'd only known Muller for a few weeks before we came aboard the *Galeskimmer*. He's not here because he wants to be. We threatened to turn him over to the Civvies if he didn't come with us. We think Muller's crimes are responsible for scaring Gilfoyle away."

"I think it's a conspiracy between Gilfoyle and Councilor Yingler," I chimed in.

"All I want to know is whether we're justified in confronting this Gilfoyle fellow," said Sable. "There's a reason you've been keeping Pyras a secret. Until I know what it is, why should I believe the rest of your story?"

"Pyras is a grav city," I said.

Mr. Scofield was dubious. "I've mapped every corner of the stream, and I've never come across such a place."

"Pyras isn't in the stream. It's in the nearflow."

Dennel McMurtry gave a loud, callous laugh. Mr. Scofield tittered. Nerimund echoed Scofield.

"That's not possible," Sable said. "Nothing survives the nearflow for long, least of all a town or a city. Any floater down there would get torn to shreds in a few days."

"Turns out surviving the nearflow is easy when you have technology from before the world shattered," I said, "not to mention gadgeteer gurus like Chester, here."

Vilaris continued, saying, "We have the ability to shield the city from inorganic matter, and a circuit of locking rods that can be disabled when we want to move. Pyras has remained a secret place for many generations, through a minimal amount of interaction with people in the stream."

Sable was beginning to understand. "You've been isolated down there since before the shattering?"

"Just after it, actually. It was only a village back then; a few families seeking refuge from the techsouls who had vowed to cleanse the world of primitives. They stayed, and now there are thousands of us."

"You're all... primitives..."

Vilaris nodded.

"How can you possibly keep that a secret?"

"It's gotten out from time to time. But of course, everyone who hears it dismisses it as a legend. Of those who do believe it, not many are willing to venture into the nearflow to look for us. And of the ones who do come looking, no one's ever developed the technology to break through our cloaking systems. We've never been found."

Sable flopped into her chair. "I don't believe it."

I smirked. "That's what I said."

"All this time, this has been about saving a city full of primitives?"

"We can survive without the money from the gravstone. But we can't survive forever without trade. There's only so much gravstone in the substrata of our floater, and we can only sell it until the surplus runs out. We lose a lot of good years if we let a delivery this big go unpaid-for."

"Well, I can't blame you for wanting your privacy," said Sable. "The few primitives I know who live in the stream have hard lives. Most of them are poor, and they deal with prejudice on a daily basis. Please realize that I don't hate you just because you're primitives. I'm not morally opposed to helping your kind; it's just dangerous keeping company with you."

"So you're still in?" asked Vilaris.

Sable glanced at her boatswain and her quartermaster. They each gave her their approval in turn. "Our arrangement stands.

We help you retrieve what belongs to you, and you help us get Uncle Angus back."

"Uncle Angus-back," said Nerimund.

"That's right, Neri," said Sable.

"Tonight, then," I said. "It happens tonight."

We spent the rest of the day finishing the last of our preparations. By mid-afternoon, the sun was hidden behind lifeless gray clouds, and a light drizzle had started. The crew was stricken with an incurable restlessness. They kept coming to me with questions about what they were supposed to do. I was losing hope that this was going to go down without something very bad happening. The fog that had cleared up by noon was returning—not as thick this time, but still a nuisance, given what my three primitive companions and I were about to do.

"I think it's time, fellas," I said, when the sun had set to a dim yellow speck, blurry behind a field of low-lying clouds. "Chaz, let's see what you've got for us."

Chaz stretched, cracked his back and neck, took off his goggles. Sweat stains darkened the chest of his shirt and the insides of his shoulders, his tied-back hair damp and oily. "They're done," he said. "Without further ado, may I present to you... the apex ingots."

He whipped a dirty rag away from the molds beside the ship's furnace. Eight round beads shone brightly within; four the size of flattened tennis balls, the other four no larger than lemons. He handed us each a set, one large and one small, and took the last pair for himself. They were smooth to the touch, their depths shot through with gleaming red-orange veins. They were perfect. Just what I'd asked him for, and just the right size—I hoped.

They were ingots of pure driftmetal.

# 9

I opened the *Galeskimmer*'s gate and stepped to the edge of the deck, my toes hanging out over empty sky. The boat was slowing, Mr. Scofield guiding her to a halt and checking his coordinates to be sure we were in the right place. The crew was gathered on the deck, sails battened down and guns in place. I clutched the center of my chest with both hands and felt the driftmetal ingots, heavy as any normal rocks in the pouch Eliza Kinally had sewn.

"Head to Platform 22 and wait for our signal," I said.

Mr. Scofield frowned at the prospect of taking orders from me, but nodded his understanding.

I flicked him an apathetic salute.

"Still sure you want to do it this way?" Vilaris asked me.

"We have to. I don't know whether Gilfoyle keeps bodyguards at his personal residence, but they'd spot the *Galeskimmer* before we got close enough to surprise them. This is the only way. We're getting your contract fulfilled, or we're taking the gravstone. There's no third scenario."

"Be careful," Vilaris said.

"It's not me you should be worried about. It's you and those weak primitive bones of yours. Better hope Chaz did the math right when he made these things."

When I looked at Chaz, the pouch strapped to his chest, and the two oddly-shaped lumps bulging out below his clavicle, I had a startling epiphany. I trusted him. That was the reason I cared about Pyras. The reason I was going to go through with this even though I could've walked away. When you trust someone—not just know them, but trust them—the idea of tying your fate to theirs becomes less daunting, somehow. Maybe I was in it for the money, too, but even selfish jerks like me like to think we do things for the right reasons every once in a while.

Chaz smiled at me, the kind of smile a person gives you when he's scared out of his mind and doesn't care that you know. I guess he trusted me too, a little.

There was worry in Sable's eyes, but hers was masked; an attempt to be brave and uncaring, even though there was more at stake than she was ready to admit. She didn't want me to know she was worried about me, but that was okay. I didn't want her to know how I really felt either.

"See you down there," I said.

I stepped overboard. I was falling, a bullet through the fog, toes pointed, arms clutching the pouch to my chest, my stomach grabbing me by the throat. *Dangit Chaz, I hope you got this right.* The pouch tried to get away from me, slipping up under my chin. I fumbled for it and held on. There was a moment when my whole body seized up like a dry engine, my mind driven wild with the thought of slamming into some unseen obstacle in the fog.

As I plunged, the larger of the two driftmetal ingots began to lighten, pulling back against the weight of my body. I had the distinct sensation of slowing, but I had no idea how fast I was going or how close I was to my destination until I saw the border lights below me, blinking through the fog.

I slowed to a halt like an elevator coming to rest in its guides, my toes scraping the roof of the building. When I started to rebound upward again I ripped open the velcro panel, releasing the larger of the two ingots. I hit the roof with as soft a clatter as I could manage, coming to rest on one knee. The ingot shot up into the clouds. A second later it came back down, bobbed up, and settled about twenty feet above me. The breeze caught it, and before I knew it the fog had wrapped it in its delicate arms and swept it away.

Chaz came next, his legs flailing to reach the roof but getting no closer to it than I had. He didn't release the ingot in time, bobbing up and down with it until he came to rest two stories up. Once he'd settled, he found himself with no choice but to let it go. He fell sideways onto the roof, landing in an unathletic heap. I caught him before he started rolling.

Vilaris followed, his timing better than either of ours. He released the ingot just as he was reaching his lowest altitude and landed on his feet, graceful as a cat. Blaylocke released too early, realized it, and grabbed the ingot with a bare fist before it got away. He tiptoed down before he let the ingot slip from his fingers and float upward into the fog. Everything happened in a matter of seconds, each of us arriving right after the last like the first snowflakes in a winter storm. They were the ugliest snowflakes I'd ever seen.

Gilfoyle's home was a glass-and-stone monstrosity of high arches and thin spires, set atop his largest grav platform like a haunted castle. The fog was clearer from the roof down, just a light mist swirling over the platform below. I couldn't see another soul from where I was. Anyone inside this wing of the house would've had to be fast asleep not to have heard us. I motioned for the others to follow as I slid down a gable and dropped onto one of the second-floor balconies, expecting to find some thug with heavy augments waiting for me.

Instead I found myself facing a glass door and a set of tall windows, peering into the bedroom on the other side. A low flame burned within an oil lamp on the dresser, casting flickering shadows over the toys strewn about the floor. A small form lay still beneath the thick yellow comforter of an overlarge bed. I checked the door. Locked.

Vilaris and the others dropped down beside me, looking about warily. Chaz knelt, produced a set of lock picks, and began to fiddle with the door. I lifted a foot to the glass and triggered my solenoid, reached through the empty space, and unlocked the door from within.

The ground crunched beneath my boots as I strode into the room and plucked the child out of bed by the pajamas. In the hallway, I saw light from downstairs. I clunked down the steps, the child tucked beneath my arm like a sack of flour. I felt her beginning to squirm as she woke up and found herself dangling above the floor. My companions' footsteps were tentative and careful behind me. They may have been whispering at me to get my attention, but I wasn't listening.

I heard voices from the kitchen as I came through the living room, its walls lined with mahogany wainscoting and built-in bookshelves. I passed the tufted oxblood sofa and its matching armchair while the cracked painting of some gray-bearded ancestor brooded over a black marble fireplace. The scent of an earlier meal grew sharper when I rounded the corner and set the child down on the tiled kitchen floor. Gilfoyle and the woman I assumed to be his wife were leaned against the counter, she in a blue silk nightgown and he in green plaid pajamas, glasses of dark red wine in their hands and an empty bottle behind them. Chaz, Vilaris, and Blaylocke waited in the living room. I could see them from where I was standing, but Gilfoyle and the woman didn't know they were there.

Gilfoyle looked at his wife. "Run. Hide." He turned his body toward me, putting himself between me and the woman. He put a hand on the counter to steady himself.

When the woman saw the child standing in front of me, tears welled in her eyes. She bent down and held out her arms, flicking her fingers inward. The little girl began to move toward her, but I grabbed her and pulled her back.

"You should ignore your husband's advice," I told the woman. "You don't want your little girl to get hurt. I don't either. You'd better stick around."

Gilfoyle was almost as brave drunk as he had been surrounded by his thugs. He held up an arm to block the woman from coming any closer to me and repeated the two words to her again. She shook her head and stood her ground, eyes darting between me and the child. The little girl was whimpering now, starting to cry.

"Everybody stays right where they are and things are gonna be fine," I said.

Gilfoyle squinted at me. "You. It's you. You're that thief. The one who tried to steal my truck."

"Wasn't the truck I was trying to steal," I said. "But never mind that. We're here to collect the money you owe the city of Pyras."

Gilfoyle looked at me like I'd just said something in another language.

"To the tune of three million chips," I continued. "Pyras has yet to see a single chip for that whole truckful of gravstone. You severed your contract with the city and took off without paying for it."

"Oh yes... it was the gravstone you wanted," Gilfoyle said. "And then my medallion."

He was wearing it. I saw the medallion's chain glinting in the light of the oil lamps, gold links against the pale skin alongside his collar.

"Sorry to be the bearer of bad news," Gilfoyle said, "but that's not what happened. Our contract expired and Lafe Yingler chose not to renew it. Then he raised the price and said he'd bring me one last shipment if I was interested. I said yes and paid him in full—exactly the price he asked."

"Which was..."

"Four million. I had no choice but to move my operation after that. Without a contract giving me exclusive rights to Pyras's gravstone, that area isn't worth mining anymore."

"*Four million* chips? Yingler jacked up the price by an entire million and you agreed? Didn't you find that weird or suspicious?"

"I didn't like paying extra, but gravstone is gravstone. You get it where you can. And as for being suspicious of Yingler, I had no reason to. I've always dealt with Lafe. He's been Pyras's go-between for as long as we've done business together. I never thought to second-guess him."

I didn't like the look of desperation in Gilfoyle's eyes. "That's a lie," I said. "You're covering your tail so you can send us on a wild goose chase and disappear again."

"Let's settle this," he said. "Let my daughter go and I'll give you whatever you want. My family has nothing to do with this situation. Leave them out of it."

I knew he was right. I released the girl's arm and let her run, sobbing, into her mother's arms. The woman fled the kitchen in the opposite direction I'd come from, into the formal dining room and down the hallway beyond.

"There. Your daughter's safe. And Pyras is out four million chips that Lafe Yingler never delivered. Give us the chips now, and you have my word that if we find four million in Yingler's possession we'll return the difference."

Gilfoyle sneered. "You expect me to part with four million chips based on the word of a common thief?"

"You said if I let your daughter go—"

"I know what I said. Takes a thief to know a thief, doesn't it? But there's one thing you didn't account for, Mr. Jakes. I will always be a better thief than you are."

"Well, naturally," I said. "I hold myself to a much lower standard."

I dove at him. He sprang onto the counter and flipped over the island. I followed in lockstep, launching myself into the air and firing my grapplewire after him. He lifted an arm to let the wire zip past his side, then sliced it in two with a single stroke, using the razor-sharp thinblade on the side of his wrist. My grappler crashed into the dining room wall, the severed length of wire whipping to a standstill behind it like a trapped snake.

Gilfoyle ducked to the side and cut across the living room. His foot slipped when he stepped up onto the coffee table. He went stumbling over the back of his oxblood sofa and landed on the hardwood floor behind it with a thud. I made a diving leap across the room, tackling him in mid-air as he was getting to his feet. He may have been wearing the medallion, but he was drunk, his reflexes slowed. We toppled to the floor and I pulled myself on top of him. I began to beat him, slamming my fist into his face until there was a rush of blue blood and the gleam of telerium-laced bone shone through on his cheeks and forehead and chin.

"Gareth... use the crackler," I heard Vilaris say.

"I can't," Blaylocke said. "I don't have it anymore. The night we escaped from Mallentis, Muller swiped the remote and destroyed it. I haven't had control of him since."

"Are you joking? He could've walked away any time he wanted? Or worse... he could've murdered us in our sleep." There was something different in Vilaris's voice. A commanding indignation I'd never heard him express before.

"He wants his share of the money first, I'm sure," Blaylocke said.

Vilaris laughed. "There's no share in any of this for him."

I stopped hitting Gilfoyle and let his head clunk to the floor. I turned around, not believing what I'd just heard. My hand was smeared with Gilfoyle's blue-violet blood. Telerium was showing through the broken skin on the tips of my knuckles. The three primitives were standing there in the living room, spectators on the far side of the sofa.

I didn't know what to say. They were speaking as if they barely knew me. Like I was some rabid animal they'd been forced to share a cage with for the past month. These weren't my friends. Why had I started to think we were alike? Humans—primitives. With red blood and brittle bones and muscles that strained and tore like paper. We weren't the same, and they'd known it for themselves all along. I saw it now: the clandestine brotherhood they shared. A brotherhood that I wasn't a part of. The three of them stood together like a flock of gossiping hens, observing me. Studying me. Judging me. I was a tool to them, after all. Only a tool.

"What did you just say?" I asked, standing.

"I said there's no share for you," Vilaris repeated. "You belong in a Regency prison, and so does the entire crew of the *Galeskimmer*."

"You're not making any sense," I said.

Gilfoyle lifted his head, eyes swollen and bloodshot behind a faceful of blood. His eyes grew wide when he saw Vilaris standing there. "Lafe?"

I looked at Vilaris again, then down at Gilfoyle.

"Hello Alastair," said Vilaris.

Gilfoyle was bewildered. "What are you doing here?"

"Renegotiating our contract."

"Hold on a minute," I said. "Vilaris, what's going on? He called you Lafe. As in, Lafe Yingler."

"You can call me Lafe too, if you'd like," Vilaris said. "It's my name. And if you let me finish, I'll tell you exactly what's going on."

Chaz and Blaylocke were backing away, putting distance between us. Had they known Vilaris and Yingler were the same person? Or had they been just as clueless as I was?

"Go right ahead," I said, holding out my bloody hand. "You just better finish with a good reason why I shouldn't do worse to you than I just did to Gilfoyle, here."

"A reason like that doesn't exist," said Vilaris... and Lafe Yingler. "You *should* want to tear me limb from limb, Muller. I never needed the crackler to control you. You've been the perfect pawn from the very beginning—a wanted man with nowhere to turn; desperate for the promise of a little coin in exchange for doing what you do best; and eager for a chance to take revenge on the man who tried to have you killed. I was lucky you fell into my lap the way you did. Years ago, when I first came to Pyras, I knew I was being given an opportunity. One I would be crazy not to take. Pyras saw the immediate effects of my presence there; I opened every avenue of trade for that city and made them more prosperous than they'd been in a hundred years. Primitives loved the idea of a techsoul who advocated for them so much that they accepted my existence without rancor. But the truth is that Lafe Yingler is more myth than man. I remained a recluse, revealing myself and exerting my influence through the persona of Clinton Vilaris. And now, thanks to you, I've become just as prosperous as the city itself. Gilfoyle *did* pay me for the gravstone. And he's about to pay me a second time… by giving it back."

"You're a maniac," I said. "Did you sabotage the *Clarity* too? Some kind of test to see whether I'd save your life?"

"Unfortunately… no. If only I were so bold and audacious as all that. I'm afraid Councilors Malwyn and DeGaffe have been plotting my demise for some time now. When we discovered the half-severed rigging lines, they were the first suspects who came to mind. I'll straighten all that out when I return to Pyras."

"What makes you think this is going to turn out in your favor?" I asked. "You'll be as wanted as I am, both in Pyras and in the stream, when the Civs find out what you've done."

"No one in Pyras will be the wiser. And as for the stream… would you mind telling me what I've done that's against the law? Did I break into the house? Did I take a hostage? Did I strike a blow, or make a threat? You did all those things, Muller. You did them very well, as a matter of fact… so well that I feel I should repay you. As thanks for your dedicated service, I've taken the liberty of reuniting you with your parents. I've also given them a gift I think will aid in that family reunion. If you'll take a look out the window, just there."

A dark shape was hovering in the fog, no more than a dozen yards from the platform. I'd know that shape anywhere. It was my ship. My *Ostelle*. A manned pulser cannon swiveled on the ship's bow in place of the old gun platform. It was swiveling in my direction.

I knelt and ripped Gilfoyle's medallion off his chest. One long dive took me through the window and sent me crashing to the platform below in a hail of shattered glass. Around my neck, the medallion latched itself to me, tiny prongs snaking deep into my skin. My body came alive with a warm, fresh feeling, like waking from sleep and clearing your sinuses and taking a dump all at once. My mind began to hum like a sewing machine, a thousand tiny impulses turning my regular thought patterns into a smooth, flowing harmony. I'd known this medallion was worth more than all the gravstone money could buy. Gilfoyle was an old man, pudgy and out of shape. He'd used the medallion to sharpen his mind more than anything. In someone who could use it to its full potential, an external mod like this could be so much more.

The first pulser burst crashed into the platform and spread across the deck. I vaulted sideways, rolling over my shoulders and back to my feet. Blue arcs raced outward from the burst before sputtering to an end, the tips crackling in my toes. *Ostelle* fired again. I dodged, not as fast this time. The outer burst caught my leg, and I felt the pinprick spiders shooting up to my knee. I cursed, hopping. Triggering my solenoid, I leapt over the side without touching the platform as the third pulser burst erupted in blue along the edge.

I was falling again, gripping the smaller chunk of driftmetal like some beloved habit I didn't want to break. The numbers appeared before long—not directly below me, but a little to my left, their blocky white lettering stark against the dark gray metal of the platform. I was slowing down again as the smaller ingot neared its altitude of equilibrium. Chaz had counterbalanced it perfectly, using careful calculations of body mass and velocity—or something like that. That's why he was the gadgeteer and I was the muscle. The *lackwit* muscle, as my dear old dad might've said. I wondered how long it was going to take dear old dad and his crew of morally-confused pirates to find me in the fog.

I came to a stop, hanging by my chest pouch like some kid trying to finish a chin-up in gym class. Platform 22 was at an inaccessible distance now that Gilfoyle had cut off my grappler. *Jerk.* And speaking of jerks, where the heck were Scofield and the *Galeskimmer*? Blaylocke was the one holding the bluewave comm we'd planned to signal them with. I still didn't know whether Blaylocke and Chaz were in on Vilaris's—Yingler's—plans. Maybe Blaylocke had told the *Galeskimmer* to leave. Maybe Vilaris had overpowered him and Chaz and done it himself. My guess was as good as mine...

Platform 22 held Gilfoyle's processing facility, a rectangle of corrugated sheet metal with a shallow roof and two smokestacks at the far end. The stuff we needed was inside. Payment or no payment, the primies weren't my concern anymore, and neither was Gilfoyle. Lafe Yingler had seen to that. From where I was sitting—or hanging, as the case may have been—they were all traitors. I had the medallion now, and I wasn't giving Vilaris/Yingler the satisfaction of another win. If anyone was going to steal that gravstone, it was me.

*I can't just hang here forever*, I told myself. *I have to make it to that platform.* I began to build momentum, tucking my legs and swinging, using the driftmetal ingot as a fulcrum. If I couldn't inch my way over to the platform, I could at least make a jump for it. And if I missed, maybe I'd be lucky enough to hit another platform on the way down.

I had built up a good tempo, my legs going almost horizontal on the upswing, when I heard engines through the fog. The high, thrumming whine of turbines, and the deep rumble of thrust. From beneath the platform, the ship's prow appeared. The point widened to its full width, emerging like a predator from its den, sliding past the battened sail and the mast, and finally to the quarterdeck, with its wheel and control array. From above I could make out the forms of the crew as if I were looking down on a set of figurines. Dennel McMurtry's top-hat and protuberant belly; Thorley Colburn, all shoulders and blond hair; Eliza Kinally's hips and wild red mane; Scofield's balding pate and faceful of snow-white; Nerimund's hunchback and pointed, drooping ears. I couldn't see Sable's thick braid or Neale Glynton's gaunt boyish frame anywhere. Something had gone wrong.

When the *Galeskimmer* was under me, I released the ingot. The deck cracked beneath my boots, straining against the force of my landing. Muffled words rang through the bluewave comm Mr. Scofield was holding up to his ear, but the turbines were so loud I couldn't make out the voice or its owner. We were in place below the facility, staring up at the wide barn doors where all the deliveries entered.

"Where are the others?" Dennel McMurtry asked, reaching out to make sure I was steady on my feet.

"Backstabbers," I said. "We have to tell Scofield... everything's changed."

I moved for the quarterdeck, but Scofield took his hand off the wheel to level a finger at me, and shouted, "Restrain that man."

"Scofield, listen to me. I'm not the one you need to worry about. Give me a minute to explain."

"Sable warned you about what would happen if you lied again," Dennel said, threatening to grab me.

"I'm not lying. Dangit, I'm not lying."

Dennel lunged at me. The medallion surged, my body harnessing its power. Before he'd gotten halfway to me, I'd slipped out of his reach and he was grabbing at empty air. Taking the quarterdeck stairs in one leap, I drew the knife from Scofield's belt and pulled the old man against me, holding the blade to his throat.

"Listen, all of you," I yelled. "I'm not going to hurt anybody. I just need a second to explain what's going on. Clinton Vilaris is not who he says he is. He isn't a primitive. He's a techsoul named Lafe Yingler who infiltrated the city of Pyras years ago and has been planning its downfall ever since. Yingler is a dangerous man. Whatever you just heard over the bluewave, Mr. Scofield, it was a lie. There's a streamboat armed with a big pulser cannon headed this way. Now, I know this is a lot to take in, but I'm not the bad guy. The man you know as Vilaris has orchestrated this entire ruse. He's the one we need to worry about. I'm going to let you go, Mr. Scofield. I apologize that I had to hold you hostage, but please... I'm on your side. They're not."

The second I released my hold on Mr. Scofield, there was a deafening crash behind me. I whirled to see the barn doors on Gilfoyle's processing facility blow open and crumple like tinfoil. A filthy black hovertruck careened through the opening, yawing sideways and skidding through the air like a bear on a frozen lake. In the driver's seat, young Neale Glynton was wide-eyed and struggling. A melee was breaking out in the truck bed as Sable attempted to hold her own against a pair of thugs with pulserods.

"You sent the Captain and the cabin boy in?" I said, shoveling a hand toward the lumbering hovertruck. "I specifically remember putting you and Thorley in charge of the breaking-in part."

Dennel shrugged. "Cap'n's orders."

I took aim with my arm, then cursed at the useless grapplewire port. *If only Chaz were here to give me a quick fix*, I thought, before remembering that Chaz was a dirty traitor. *Screw Chaz*, I corrected myself. I darted forward, leapt down the stairs, and ran along the deck toward the bow, following the hovertruck as it sped along overhead. I was going to make a jump for it, and there would be no second *Galeskimmer* to break my fall this time.

The hovertruck dipped as Neale struggled with the controls, dropping in so close I could smell the displacer engines and feel their heat on the top of my head. The vehicle zoomed past just as I reached the bow.

Solenoid.

I was flying toward it with a little extra in my jump, and then the hovertruck dipped again and I was too high, soaring over the top and watching the thugs begin to beat Sable to the floor of the truck bed with their pulserods.

I spun the cylinder in my arm—not the one with the grapplewire; the left arm, with the darts. I locked in a good one, the readout in my enhanced eye telling me what I was dealing with. I flicked my wrist back, and the dart shot through the top of the thug's skull. My body was flipping as I flew past the truck bed and lost sight of them, crashing onto the hovertruck's hood like a thrown wrestler. Little boy Neale smiled at me and gave the controls an excited yank. I bounced up and slammed down hard again. Good thing I wasn't a primie, or I might've broken something.

Where the hood met the windshield, I clung by the tips of my fingers and tried to get to one knee. We were swaying as we flew. I could hear Sable's gasps and feel the pulserod zapping her, missed strokes gonging the metal bed and vibrating through the truck. I lifted myself and ran up the hood, letting the truck's velocity carry me over the windshield and across the roof. I spun around and laid out, driving my shining telerium wrist spikes through the thug's shoulders and dragging him along with me.

We crashed down next to the motionless body of the other thug, the one I'd hit with the dart. The live thug fought back all the harder as I plunged my spikes into his face and chest. He was alternating clumsy swings between the pulserod and a closed fist when he caught me on the shoulder. Just a glancing blow, but with a pulserod, even a glancing blow is enough.

The prickling wave jolted through me. I slumped over, mashing my face against the truck bed. The thug climbed to his feet, rivulets of purplish blood streaming from his puncture wounds like runoff from a sewer drain. Sable groaned and rolled over, still dazed and waiting to regain control of her body. My vision flashed white as the pulserod crashed into the back of my skull, its electric echo radiating through me. The thug reeled back and swung again, bashing my ribcage with another shocking blow.

Neale must have decided we were getting too far away from the *Galeskimmer*, because the hovertruck twisted around and everyone slid across the bed like crackers on a fast-moving plate. Cumbersome as these hovertrucks were, the ability of centrifugal force to part your feet from the ground is not something to underestimate. The thug toppled over me, his pulserod spinning away across the bed. I slid toward the back edge; the dead thug slid into me, and Sable into him.

We were headed back toward the *Galeskimmer* now, picking up speed but not flying high enough to clear the mast when we got there. If little Neale Glynton wasn't driving fast enough to snap the mast in half, he was going to wrap this truck around it like a breakfast omelet. I was less worried about our flight path than about the thug who was picking himself up at the back of the truck bed. He had a plasticky face and robotic hands—exposed telerium digits, tension hinges, and optical fibers snaking down his arms. Sable and I were getting to our feet too. Now it was two against one. But that didn't matter much, seeing as our ride was about to come to an abrupt end.

What bothered me most, however, was that beyond the far side of Platform 22, the shape of my *Ostelle* was emerging from the fog.

# 10

I shot the frayed end of my grapplewire into my opposite hand, holding it like I was getting ready to floss a giant's teeth. Sable began to circle the tiny truck bed, knifeblade at the ready. The thug eyed the pulserod lapping at his heels, judging whether we'd let him crouch for it. No, he decided, and backed up a step to activate his knucklespurs. They slammed out from his clenched robotic fists with a metallic stomping sound, miniature telerium pyramids that made his hands look like dog collars.

We were speeding toward the *Galeskimmer*. I didn't have time for this nonsense. I feinted with the grapplewire. The thug flinched. I shot him with a dart, the same kind I'd used to put a hole in his buddy's skull. He plucked it from his chest and tossed it behind him, a smug look on his punctured, bloody face. Then his look turned sour. He staggered, buckled over, and flopped off the rear edge of the truck bed.

Sable breathed a sigh of relief. We turned and peered over the front lip of the truck bed to see where we were headed. The *Galeskimmer* had docked itself below the crumpled doors of the processing facility. Thorley and Dennel were inside, tossing chunky burlap sacks into the growing dust cloud they'd started on the *Galeskimmer*'s deck. My *Ostelle* was coming across the port side, leveling the pulser cannon and making ready to fire. Carrying gravstone on a ship that flies on driftmetal runners is a bad idea of the most monumental kind. But hey, what other option did we have?

I vaulted onto the hovertruck's roof, swung down onto the running board, and cracked the door to pull myself inside. "Where'd you learn to drive, the bloody circus?" I said.

Neale might have blushed, but he was already so red in the face I couldn't tell the difference. He gave me the slightest shrug. He was tiptoeing the pedals from the edge of the seat, his chin lifted so he could see over the steering column.

"It hovers," I said, grabbing his hand and easing the controls into their neutral position. "You don't have to stay moving all the time. Press the right pedal and let the left one come toward you 'til they're even. Good, now drop the displacers flat."

Neale obeyed, bringing the truck to an awkward standstill. I motioned for him to switch places with me. When he crawled past me on the seat, he mopped cold sweat across the back of my shirt. I slid into place at the controls and tipped us forward, shouting through the window for Sable to hold onto her hat. A pulser round spidered across the *Galeskimmer*'s hull as we approached, rocking the boat on its runners. On the quarterdeck, Mr. Scofield looked over his shoulder in shocked surprise to see my *Ostelle* creeping from the fog like a phantom.

I eased the hovertruck to a stop beside the *Galeskimmer*. "Change of plans," I shouted. "Get off the truck, you two. Get your boat out of here as quick as you can."

Sable and Neale hopped onto the streamboat. "What are you about to do?" Sable asked, eyeing me.

I would've told her, if there were a chance she would've agreed to it. "Just get out of here."

I veered away and took off toward my *Ostelle*, determined to distract the law-lovers I called parents for as long as I had to. I swerved into a sideways strafe, the closest thing to an evasive maneuver I could manage in this crippled turd of a hovertruck. The pulser cannon drew a bead on my lame tricks without breaking a sweat, but no shots came my way. Instead, the turret shifted its gaze onto the *Galeskimmer* and fired. The pulser hit one of the turbines, rattling the whole boat like a beggar's cup. In light of my distraction's apparent ineffectiveness, I gunned it straight ahead.

"I'm sorry baby," I muttered, taking one last look at my beautiful undamaged *Ostelle* as she came zooming up to life size. "I'm so sorry."

I aimed for center mass, unconcerned with where I landed, as long as I struck her a good one. I felt like an abusive lover, treating my pride and joy like the wall at a bumper car rink.

The hovertruck smashed into the deck head-on. The air outside my windshield was a mist of splinters and rivets and men I knew, screaming and diving to get out of the way. I was ploughing through layers of decking I'd laid down myself, sweating away in the afternoon sun with a rivetgun and a dream. I wondered if it was really worth it to send my parents and I and their whole crew to the Churn, all for a girl I only kind of knew, and half a dozen other less-endearing souls who were about to steal the fortune that should've been mine.

It wasn't, I decided. It wasn't worth it at all.

The hovertruck's nose accordioned. Then the whole truck began to flip forward and vault away from the deck, like a fat gymnast attempting a somersault. I gripped the steering controls and locked my arms and legs as the truck inverted itself. I was sailing past a blur of debris toward midship, and the whole world was turning upside down. All I could think was, *I'm never gonna get to tell anyone how awesome this is.*

I was facing a sleeping bat's version of the direction I'd come from when the hovertruck smashed into what I knew must've been the hatch in front of the center mast. The sudden stop sent a wave of pain down my spine. I slid off my seat and onto the windshield, smacking my head against something on the way down. I could see belowdecks through the huge hole the hovertruck had ripped in the floor. But my *Ostelle* was still afloat. Still standing proud. There had been no explosion; I'd achieved no glorious, heroic ending. That meant I still had work to do.

I kicked open the driver's side door and flopped onto the deck, ears ringing, head and back smarting. I shot my last dart into Johnny Ralston's right eye as he came toward me. I didn't know for sure he was intent on violence, but the way I saw it, everyone on board my ship was the enemy. After all, they'd helped kick me off it.

I stumbled toward the pulser cannon, watching as the barrel spit another burst into the *Galeskimmer*'s backside. I felt more crewmembers converging on me, the way you feel every pair of eyes on a dark street.

Launching myself the last several yards, I slung my grapplewire around the gunner's neck and yanked him out of the turret chair. It was Norris Ponting, a skilled powder monkey if ever there was one. Norris Ponting was about to become a 'was,' unless I got my way. I whirled on the advancing crew and shouted, "Stop right where you are, all of you, or Norris is done for."

They did stop, but I got the impression that most of them were considering whether Norris was worth stopping for. As long as they spent some time deciding, that was fine by me; all I had to do was keep them off that pulser cannon long enough to let the *Galeskimmer* make a run for it. My grapplewire was tight around Norris's throat, tight enough to make every breath come out wheezing. He was half-drunk, by the smell of him. I'd have bet money he was still a better shot than any other two crewmembers put together.

Knowing the whole crew on a first-name basis meant that I knew their tech, too. I knew who was augmented and who wasn't, where their augments were, and how they were likely to use them. I backed toward the turret with them inching toward me, ravenous as a pack of wild dogs. Ma and Dad were nowhere to be seen. I guessed Dad was at the helm, past the hovertruck that was sticking fifteen feet into the air at midship, three of its four engines still idling.

When my back rubbed against the turret chair, I yanked Norris Ponting around the side with me and sat down in it. I pulled him across my lap so I could reach the controls. We swiveled around in a one-eighty so the pulser cannon was pointed straight at the hovertruck. I was a little surprised the gun had the capability to turn that far, but I wasn't complaining.

Norris Ponting was getting squirmy. I had the pulser cannon as collateral now; I didn't need him anymore. So I planted a foot in his back and shoved him over the railing. He cried out as he fell. One or two of the crew jerked forward, but thought better of coming any closer. Over my shoulder, the *Galeskimmer* was making ready to cast off. Another twenty seconds, I judged, and she would be on her way toward clearer skies. That was when Yingler emerged from belowdecks, picking his way up the staircase's wreckage and appearing from behind the hovertruck.

"I wouldn't be so hasty," shouted the man formerly known as Vilaris.

"Knowing you're on board is all the incentive I need," I said, rubbing the trigger button with my thumb.

"There's something you should be made aware of, Muller."

"I'm already aware that killing you is going to make me very happy," I said. I eased the controls. The turret swiveled until I had Yingler in the gun sights.

"Be that as it may... don't look down. Or rather... do."

I did. Half a dozen sloops were rising through the fog below my *Ostelle*, all of them flying the red-and-tan flag of the Civil Regency Corps. The Civs had cast electronets between their ships like a collage of spider webs. *To catch me in case I try to jump again*, I realized. Norris Ponting was in the closest of the nets, climbing aboard the nearest sloop with help from the Civs.

This Yingler was a real piece of work. Not only had he managed to befriend my parents; the scheming wretch was bold enough to show his face to the Civs like they weren't going to lock him up for what he'd done. Sable and her crew were getting ready to take the money and run, leaving me here to fend for myself after I'd led them to the jackpot of a lifetime. And don't get me started on how I felt about my parents.

I'd had it with trusting people, I decided. I'd had it with civility. This was war—even if I was the only person on my side. Even if I was pitting myself against a world full of people who were against me.

I pressed the trigger. Yingler erupted in blue arcs of electromagnetic energy that shot to his feet and spread out across the deck. People dove for cover, unsheathed their weapons, and began to fire them at me. Before Yingler had slumped paralyzed to the deck, I was already swiveling to face the Civs. I trained my sights on the sloop Norris Ponting had climbed into, and fired. The sloops were small; lighter and faster than streamboats like the *Galeskimmer* and my *Ostelle*. One pulser shot from above carried enough burst to cover almost the entire deck and fry every techsoul on board.

I swiveled toward the next sloop and followed up with another well-placed shot. Every member of the crew went stiff as a tree trunk and fell over. The clinkers on the first sloop were going haywire, and the boat shot upward as the driftmetal runners exerted their unchecked force. The electronets broke away, but not before pulling an adjacent sloop so far up that half the crew went sliding over the port railing. I didn't stop until I'd disrupted every Civvy ship in sight. Bullets and laser bolts and flecker rounds were pummeling the back of the armored turret chair.

I was creating chaos, and loving every second of it.

Then someone managed to hit the pulser cannon with a hand pulser. It surged and went dead. At Platform 22, the *Galeskimmer* was setting off. I had half a mind to shoot it, too. It was a good thing the cannon was out of commission, because as soon as the *Galeskimmer* left the dock, it turned around and came toward me.

Sable was at the helm, with Dennel and Thorley and Mr. Scofield and Nerimund manning the four-pounders. They loosed a volley in our direction. The air rushed past my head and the cannonballs crashed and bounded across the deck. They reloaded and fired once more before Sable straightened her out and came across the bow. My parents' crew was shooting at the *Galeskimmer* now. Eliza Kinally and Neale Glynton were returning fire with a pair of old muskets.

Sable eased the *Galeskimmer* into place beside us and shouted at me above the din. "Are you just gonna sit there, or do you want a lift?"

I didn't think twice. I leapt onto the *Galeskimmer* and rolled behind a stack of crates as she idled past. Sable released the clinkers and took us straight up into the fog, the whole ship rocking and lurching amid a hail of disruptive gunfire. Then I heard something ping into one of the turbines and go clattering around inside it.

A thousand failing brakes screeched. There was a rush of heat, a fireball, and the sensation of being tossed around like pasta in a strainer.

When the ship stabilized, we were still rocketing upward through the fog. Something had hit me on the head, and I could see only blue-violet out of my unenhanced eye. The deck was a wreckage of bodies and burning wood, and when I tried to stand, the force of the ship's upward momentum kept me on my hands and knees. *Sweet merciful Leridote, how many shipwrecks am I gonna be involved in this month?* I rolled onto my back and stared at the approaching heights, the mast and the furled sail flapping from the yardarm, until it all went from dark and foggy to nothing but black.

I dreamed at hyperspeed, so I knew I was still alive. I dreamed about Kupfer and Sable and Ma and Dad and Yingler and the shop, and all my kid friends back home in Atherion. I dreamed that Blaylocke was burning alive and Gilfoyle's daughter was dancing around the flames, singing nursery rhymes, drinking red wine and wearing her bright yellow blanket as a cape. I dreamed my augments were coming alive and building mechanical spiders out of the synthetic tissues of my arms and legs. When my limbs were gone, Chaz was controlling the whole thing, orchestrating it with a remote control in his laboratory, talking to the spiders.

I dreamed the medallion was putting ideas into my head, making me paranoid and forcing me to believe I was a wanted criminal. But it was Sable's Uncle Angus—Uncle Angus, whom I'd never met, but who my mind made an image of—plotting at Maclin Automation to commit my crimes for me and drop pamphlets over every floater in the stream telling people about how I ate children and stole loose change from old ladies and put embarrassing clothing on defenseless statues.

I was staring at the same mast and the same furled sail when I woke up. The sky above was bright and blue, and the fires I'd fallen asleep to had become smoldering pillars of smoke. I stood. We were very high up; the air that was filtering into my lungs was thin and cold and crisp. I was used to air like this. I'd grown up on a floater that was even higher in the stream. The medallion was burning on my chest, its frantic algorithms racing across my mind.

Sable was beside me, her hand on my back. "Are you okay?" she was asking. "I didn't want to move you. I didn't know how bad you'd been hurt, so I made sure you were breathing and I let you sleep."

I turned to her. Her eyes were red-rimmed and her cheeks were flushed. "Where are we?"

"Somewhere above the Kalican Heights. It's bad. The ship's completely disabled. One of the turbines is blown to shreds. All the clinkers but one on the starboard side are ruined. Neale and Eliza were on that side of the ship when it blew. They're both hurt bad, but I think they'll be okay. But Landon is... Mr. Scofield..." She couldn't get another word out.

"I'm sorry," I said. "It's my fault. You came back to get me. You should've left me on my own to face what I had coming. None of this would've happened."

"Don't," she managed, holding up a hand. "I can't."

I took her into my arms, held her. The gesture felt awkward and stilted to me, but Sable didn't seem to think so. She buried her face in my jacket and whimpered, the kind of thing a child does after they've been crying for a long time and there isn't much steam left. We stood like that for a while until she pulled away.

"You're glad we came back for you though. Aren't you?"

I allowed myself half a smile. "I'm a little confused as to why."

She gave me a weepy grin. "That makes two of us."

I laughed. "It's so you'd have someone to be mean to. That's why you wanted me around."

"I'm the captain. Being mean is what captains do."

"Well then, Captain. I suggest you start giving some orders. The wind's picking up. Just because we have one bad engine doesn't mean we can't set sail. We're filthy rich now, you know. Getting this rig fixed up shouldn't take more than a few days once we find ourselves a nice secluded floater."

"Fine," she said. "Then hop on the bluewave and start mapping me some coordinates. Thorley, get up on that yardarm and set the mainsail. Mr. McMurtry, take the controls. I'll tend to the wounded for now. Move it, all of you!"

We would've sailed off into the sunset, but that's not where the stream was taking us. I knew one day I'd have to face my parents again. I'd probably have to face Kupfer, and Yingler too. Chaz, who I'd liked, but now hated for betraying me—and Blaylocke, who I'd hated but actually started to like... before realizing I'd been right to hate him all along. I'd have to face them *all* again someday. But for now, the only thing that mattered was that I was a free man. I was a free man in a world that didn't think I deserved to be. And despite all the terrible garbage I'd been through—that this crew and I had been through—we were sailing on driftmetal runners with the clouds in our hair. And that was a damned good feeling.

Printed in Great Britain
by Amazon.co.uk, Ltd.,
Marston Gate.